The Rancher's Mail Order Bride

by Kirsten Osbourne

The Rancher's Mail Order Bride

by Kirsten Osbourne

Book Two in the Dalton Brides Series

Copyright ©2014 Kirsten Osbourne

License Notes

Table of Contents

The Rancher's Mail Order Bride by Kirsten Osbourne   1

Foreword

Through no fault of her own, Gwen Blue found herself embroiled in a scandal that would set Beckham, Massachusetts on its ear, and get her locked in her room for two months. When she found herself betrothed to a man she found loathsome, she wanted nothing more than to disappear. When her sisters liberated her from her room and proposed a journey to Texas to visit an old school friend, she didn't have to be asked twice.

Walton Dalton always had a plan for his life. He'd spent years learning everything he needed to know about ranching, and he had a large parcel of land adjacent to his two brothers' land. Between the three of them, they were going to build a Texas ranching empire. For his empire, he needed a bride.

Without his brothers' knowledge, Walt sends off for three mail order brides from a matchmaker in Beckham. He knows from the moment he sees 'Gorgeous Gwen' that she's meant to be his. Will she agree to the marriage? If she does, will she be able to get over her self-centered attitude and be a good wife?

The Brothers

Walton Dalton stood in the middle of his land, knowing he'd found his place in the world. The two sections next to his were both open, and he was staking claim for his brothers. The three of them would own a huge section of Texas dirt, and they would ranch it together.

Walton was the oldest of three brothers. They didn't like to be reminded that he was the oldest though. With only fifteen minutes difference between him and his brother, Nate, and twenty-five minutes between him and Bart, they preferred to all think of themselves as the same age. They weren't though. Walton was always aware of his burden as the eldest. He had to be the strongest, fastest and best of the three, so that he could live up to what was expected of him.

He hadn't built his house yet, so he sat down right there in the dirt to write letters to his brothers, asking them to join him. He knew they would. He'd always been the ringleader of the three of them, and even as adults, he was certain he could convince them ranching was the way for them to gain wealth and happiness.

Rather than writing two different letters, he just wrote one and copied it for the other. When he was finished, he had two letters that read the same.

My Dear Brother,

I'm writing you from a section of land that I'm about to begin homesteading in north Texas. The two sections beside me are available. I'd like for the three of us to claim this land and build a ranching empire here in the Lone Star State. We could have land for as far as the eye can see, and the prairie here is so flat you can see a long way.

I'm about a half day's ride south of a town called Weatherford, which is west of Fort Worth. If you get to the area, people will know me. No one forgets a Dalton.

I hope you'll consider joining me here, because I need you both. There's enough work for twenty men, but between the three of us, I know we can do the work of thirty. Remember what Pa always said? "When you three team up, nothing can stop you." The local ranchers won't know what hit them once the Dalton brothers make their mark.

I'm going to start building my cabin. When you two get here, we'll build a couple more houses and get us some ladies. It's time.

Don't take too long to get here. Land is

going fast.

Sincerely,

Walt

He folded both of the letters and got to his feet. His spirited stallion danced away from him, as if he was trying to get him to not settle down. "We're here to stay, Spirit. No more wandering for us."

Walton and Spirit had done more than their share of traveling. He had spent the last ten years as a cowboy, learning the ins and outs of ranching. He was finally ready to start a life, and he was going to do it.

He swung up onto Spirit and rode him into town. It was an hour to the closest small town of Wiggieville, but he knew that with his two brothers' help, they would soon have a bustling town right there. He could picture it already.

*****

For the life of him, Bart Dalton couldn't figure out how his brother Walt had tracked him down. He'd only ridden into the bustling city of San Francisco the day before, after all, and hadn't even planned on stopping there. How in high heaven did Walt know to send a letter to the San Francisco post office before Bart even knew he was going there?

Bart had been on his way from running an apple-picking crew in the Yakima River Valley in the Washington Territory to a new California village called Hollywood when he hooked up with a couple of other drifters like himself. They said they were headed for Frisco, so he tagged along. It wasn't like he had any pressing business in Hollywood, he just thought the name sounded nice. He could almost see massive groves of holly trees surrounding the little community.

As he thought back on his last letter to his brothers — he always wrote one and just copied it for the other — he recalled saying something about California. But that was months ago. As far as Walt and Nate knew, he could have come and gone by then.

But it had always been like that with them. No matter how much distance separated them, they always seemed to know in their gut what was happening with the others. Like that time Walt got bucked from a horse he was trying to break and got a concussion.

Bart had been dealing faro in a Kansas City gambling hell at the time, and an overwhelming urge to sleep came over him. Somehow he knew Walt had been injured so he walked right out of that hell, jumped on his trusty horse Roamer, and rode east in the direction of St. Louis.

By the time he arrived several days later, Walt was up and around, and didn't seem the least bit surprised Bart had shown up. Nate arrived a few hours later. They all had a good laugh, and spent a few days reminiscing and catching up before Bart's feet started itching to get back on the road. That was the last time he'd seen his brothers, and he missed them something fierce.

Being triplets, they'd always been close but, aside from his brothers, no one ever let Bart forget he was the youngest, even though it was only by minutes. Walt was the bossy older brother and Nate was the no-nonsense one. Everyone expected Bart to be the wild one of the bunch, the irresponsible younger brother, and he was all too happy to oblige.

He'd get into all sorts of trouble and blame it on his brothers. Of course, they did the same to him, so it evened out in the end. He pretended it was all in good fun, but deep down he felt empty, like something was missing. It was like he hadn't yet found his true identity, and everyone's expectations — or lack of them — were holding him back from discovering it.

As he and his brothers grew older, he felt stifled at his family home in Oregon City. His brothers seemed perfectly content helping out around the dairy farm, but Bart knew there was so much more out in the world than milking cows and shoveling manure. He wanted to see it all. Maybe once he saw everything there was to see, he'd settle down and live a 'normal' life, but until that day, he'd never be truly happy.

The day after their seventeenth birthday, Bart woke up ready to break the news to his brothers: He was leaving and didn't know when or if he'd ever see them again. He was giddy with excitement but also heartbroken at the idea of leaving them.

They were a part of him and he was having trouble imagining life without them, but he had to do this. As much as he wanted them to come with him, he had to strike out on his own and find that elusive thing that was missing from his soul.

His gut churned as he crept through the quiet house in the early morning hours. He'd get Roamer saddled and packed, then go wake his brothers. If he was lucky, he'd be able to sneak away without waking his folks. Ma would have a fit and Pa might refuse to let him go. He longed to say goodbye but it would be too risky.

Stepping into the barn, he was stopped in his tracks by the sight of his entire family — Ma, Pa, Walt and Nate — standing around an already-saddled and fully loaded Roamer. Tears were streaming down Ma's plump cheeks, and Pa had a comforting arm wrapped around her shoulders. Walt had a worried look on his face and Nate just looked irritated. Only Pa was smiling, even though it held a twinge of sadness.

"How did you know?" Bart stammered in surprise.

Pa tilted his head at Walt and Nate. "Your brothers told us. You didn't tell them?" He chuckled and shook his head. "Figgers."

"I packed you several days worth of food," sniffled his mother. "Don't eat it all at once. I can't stand the thought of you starving out on the trail."

"Yes, Ma," he whispered, humbled at his family's support and love. Why hadn't he trusted that they would understand?

Walt sidled up to him and slapped him on

the back. "You'll be fine out there, Bart, but you know if you ever need anything, me and Nate are here for ya."

"I know, brother."

As irritated as Nate looked, he still pulled Bart into a fierce hug. "Don't be stupid."

Bart smiled. It was an old joke between them, going back to when they were little kids. He returned his brother's hug, and soon his whole family had their arms wrapped around him.

Pa was the first to pull away. Clearing his throat of emotion, he croaked, "Sun's fixing to come up, son. Best you get while the getting's good."

Bart gritted his teeth as he rode out of the barn, willing himself to not look back. If he looked back, he might change his mind, and the last thing he wanted was to be stuck in Oregon City for the rest of his life.

Leaving his family behind was the hardest thing he'd ever had to do. And in the ten years he'd spent rambling around the country, it remained at the top of the list.

Rereading Walt's letter, Bart bristled a bit at the commanding tone. Walt always assumed the others would do whatever he told them to, like he was their ringleader or something simply by virtue of being a few minutes older. Bart had spent much of his youth rebelling against his oldest brother's overbearing ways, and he was amused to find the instinct was still there. Some things never changed.

"Whatcha got there, Bart?"

Bart was startled out of his reverie by one of his latest riding companions. Chuck was his name, and he was as shifty a drifter as Bart had ever met. And he'd met a lot. He would never dream of doing business with the man, but Chuck was pleasant enough to pass the time with on the trail.

"Oh, just a letter from my brother, inviting me to settle near him in Texas," Bart replied, carefully folding the letter and slipping it into an inner pocket he'd had sewn into his duster.

"Oh, yeah?" Chuck's eyes sparkled as he leaned back against the wall of the post office next to Bart. "I hear they're giving away land left and right out there. Whereabouts is he settling?"

There was an unspoken code among drifters like them: Never ask personal questions. Too many men were running from something, and all were suspicious by nature, so it was best to keep your questions to yourself.

Obviously Chuck hadn't learned that lesson yet.

"North, I think," Bart evaded.

Chuck took the hint and nodded sagely, as if that explained everything. "You goin'?"

The man's question took him by surprise. He honestly hadn't even thought about it. He'd been too wrapped up in memories.

"I dunno." And he really didn't. He'd been moving around so much over the years that he didn't think he'd know how to sit still for very long, even if he was so inclined.

Which he wasn't.

But something tugged at his insides, remembering the day he rode away from his family. He'd do anything for them, and now Walt was asking for his help. *I hope you'll consider joining me here, because I need you both.* That was as close to begging as Walt ever got.

Bart was honestly surprised that his brothers hadn't married and settled down by now. They'd both always been more traditional and down-to-earth than he had ever dreamed of being — or ever wanted to be.

But at 27, they were a bit overdue in starting their own families. He ached for them a little because they'd both always talked about having a bunch of young'uns running around. He didn't really understand it but he felt bad for them that they didn't have it yet.

Resolve settled in his belly like a glowing coal. His brothers would do anything for him, and had already helped him out of more jams than he cared to think about. Walt was right; it was time. Time to return the favor.

He'd ride out to Texas and help Walt and Nate set up their ranch, even if it took a year or two. It was the least he could do. When everything was rolling along, and his brothers had a couple of nice wives — maybe even some babies — he'd leave his portion to them and continue his search for whatever was missing in his life.

"'Scuse me," he mumbled to Chuck and strode back into the post office.

Walt,

You can count on me, brother.

Bart

*****

"Get him, Nate!"

A growing crowd of townspeople and cowhands cheered as Nate Dalton landed face first in the dirt. He rolled to his back and, with lightning speed — at least it felt like it, considering the blow he'd been dealt — climbed to his feet to face his opponent. The dirty chuck-eater clobbered him with a piece of firewood, and even now held it before him like a shield.

"Seems we have a difference of opinion," Nate told him as he wiped away the blood trickling down one side of his face. This had to be the worst cattle drive he'd ever been on.

The Easterner, a man Nate figured had no business changing the price per head, swallowed hard and raised the wood as if to hit him again. The difference was, this time he faced Nate instead of sneaking up on him like he did when he'd struck him the first time.

"As Mr. Meyer's du...duly... appointed representative..." he stammered, "I must ask you to concede to the new price given."

Nate shook his head against a bout of dizziness, and hoped he didn't have a concussion like the one his brother Walt did a few years back. For a scant second he wondered if his two brothers would show up to check on him as they'd done for Walt.

The thought was lost however when the good-for-nothing dandy took another swing at him. Nate ducked and dodged, and blocked the next blow with one fist as he punched the low-life in the face with the other to send him sprawling. "I'll do my business with Mr. Meyers, if you don't mind."

The man didn't get up. In fact, he didn't respond at all. Nate stared at him a moment as Sam Wheeler, one of his drovers, slapped him on the back. "You showed him!"

Nate leaned forward and peered at the unconscious form. At least he hoped he was unconscious. He didn't hit him that hard, did he? "Where's Meyers? How come he sent this idiot for me to deal with?"

"He's at his ranch. I hear tell from folks down at the post office his wife is having a baby. That's why this yellow-belly is in town."

"This yellow-belly tried to gouge the price per head. Now I'll have to ride out to the Meyers' ranch to get our business done."

Sam looked at the man on the ground. A couple of their fellow cowboys tried to get him to come around by slapping the side of his face a few times. "Maybe you should take this fool back with ya and tell Mr. Meyers what he did?"

"Won't have to," Nate said. "This is a small town, with enough people here to let Meyers know what happened. I'll wager this duffer to be out of a job come suppertime."

"Oh, good point," said Sam as he reached into his pocket. "I almost forgot, here's a letter for ya."

"A letter?"

"Yeah, it's from your brother. He wants ya to come to Texas."

Nate's eyes narrowed. "You read my

mail?"

"No help for it! There's a tear in the envelope, see?" he said and pointed. "Is it my fault if'n the letter fell out?"

Nate rolled his eyes and shook his head in exasperation. It hurt. He winced as he touched his wound and blinked a few times to clear his vision. He was tired of dealing with ranchers who didn't know how to run their business or make a good profit. He hoped whatever Walt wrote didn't add to an already disastrous cattle drive. He unfolded the letter and studied it, but the words were too blurry for him to read. Not a good sign.

"Looks like the dandy got ya a good one," said the grizzled cowhand as he stared at Nate's head. "Want me to read your letter for ya?"

"I'll be fine, go make sure that idiot is still alive, will ya? And then tell the rest of the boys to wait for me. I'll be back."

"Where ya goin'?"

"Post office." He strode past Sam and headed down the street. He didn't get far when another bout of dizziness hit, and he slowed his pace to keep from falling over. He'd been hit in the head before, be it from a fist, a kick, or the occasional hard object, but this particular hit, coupled with Walt's letter, managed to do something Nate hadn't yet. It knocked some sense into him. "Sense" being the operative word.

Nate used to have his share of good sense at one time, the type other men respected and sought out so they could benefit too. Nate, being as sensible as he was, gave his advice freely. Not only did he give it, he was willing to receive it.

Except for a piece of advice given him by his last employer, one Thomas Adams, who advised Nate to stay away from his daughters, or else. The "or else" meant Nate would decorate a cottonwood come morning if Mr. Adams found any of his precious daughters compromised.

Nate wasn't stupid and, lucky for him, wasn't attracted to any of the four women. This made it easy to stay away from them. Keeping them away from him, on the other hand, was another matter.

Two of them snuck into the bunkhouse one night. A third rode out to where he and some of the men were branding cattle. If he'd listened to his good sense, he'd have high-tailed it off the Adams' spread pronto. But no… Instead, Lucretia, the fourth and most aggressive of the bunch, launched herself at him the same night in the foyer of the ranch house. She flung her arms around his neck and kissed him as her father came down the stairs.

Nate barely escaped with his life.

But his ordeal with the Adams sisters was behind him, and he wanted to keep it that way. If there was one thing he couldn't stand, it was a forward female trying to rope him into matrimony. He would marry when he was good and ready, not to mention settle down.

Nate reached the post office and leaned against the door a moment before going in. By now his head throbbed something awful. He unfolded Walton's letter and took another stab at reading it. It wasn't easy, but he managed. After several moments he refolded the missive and stuck it back into a shirt pocket.

"Texas," he muttered to himself. "Looks like you found yourself a sweet deal, big brother." But was he ready to join him?

"Good Lord!" A woman cried to his left. "What happened to you?"

Nate stared at her, a bemused look on his face. She pointed to his head and gasped. "Oh, yeah. Sorry ma'am. I...got cut ...shaving."

The woman shook her head and made a tsk, tsk, tsk, sound. "You'd best get that taken care of. What were you doing? Trying to shave your head with an ax?"

"A piece of wood, actually," Nate said drily. "Bad barber." He turned and headed for the postmaster.

"Yes?" said a wiry little man behind the counter. He peered at Nate over his spectacles and gasped louder than the woman. "Egad! You're bleeding!"

"I've been informed. Do you have any other mail for me? The name's Nate Dalton." It would be like Sam to bring only the one letter and leave everything else. The postmaster grimaced one more time before he turned to search for any remaining mail.

Nate and the other drovers only came to Fountain, Colorado once every couple of months. As it was more frequent than other places he'd been cow punching, it was as good a place as any to have his mail sent.

"No sir, Mr. Dalton," the postmaster announced as he turned around. "Nothing else here. Lucky you came into town when you did, that letter arrived only a week ago."

"Much obliged," said Nate as he turned and headed for the door. As he stepped onto the boardwalk a thought struck. After he sold his employer's stock, collected the money, and headed back, he wouldn't have another chance to answer Walton's letter until the next time they brought in more cattle.

He stared at the dirt in the street in

indecision. He could still taste the same dirt in his mouth. He let out a weary sigh, took his brother's letter out of his pocket, and stared at it a moment.

"Texas ..." he mused. Walt wanted to settle down, start an empire, not to mention a family. Was he ready to do that?

A man crossing the street caught Nate's eye. The man was heading toward the post office. Nate reached out and stopped him before he could go inside. "Hey mister, where's the doctor in this town?"

"Go down to the end of the street, turn left, and you'll find him. I think he just got back from the Meyers' ranch." He looked at Nate and let out a low whistle. "I think you'd best hurry and have him tend ya." The man shuddered, pulled out of Nate's hold, and went into the post office.

Nate watched him go, before he looked in

the direction he'd indicated. As he started off, he wondered if Bart answered their brother yet. Would he be ready to settle down? Of the three, Bart had the worst case of itchy feet.

Nate could wander as well as the next, but he at least stuck in one place for a while before moving on. Sometimes he'd stay in one spot a couple of years. Bart was lucky to stay in one place a couple of months. But in his gut, Nate knew Bart had answered their brother's call.

He reached the doctor's house, stuffed Walt's letter into his pocket again, and went inside.

"Jumpin' Jehoshaphat!" An elderly man cried when he saw him. "What happened to you?"

"Never mind, are you the doctor?" asked Nate. "I need me a piece of paper and something to write with. I got a letter here needs answering."

"Letter? I'd say let it wait, son. That gash on your forehead needs tendin'. Let me get a few things and I'll fix ya right up."

"My letter needs tending more than I do."

"What's so important it can't wait until after I fix your wound?"

Nate gave him a broad smile. "Cause I gotta let my big brother know I'm gonna settle in Texas!"

The doctor gawked at him, shook his head, and went to fetch him paper, pen, and ink.

Dear Walt,
Count me in.
Nate

*****

Walton worked hard to build a small house while he waited for his brothers' replies. Twice a week he would ride into town for fresh supplies and see if there were any new letters.

Finally, more than a month after he'd mailed his letters there was one from Bart. Walton read it right there in the store and smiled. One of his brothers would be there any day, and they'd start building their empire. The Daltons were going make their mark on Texas.

It took another week before he received a later from Nate. He was coming, too. All of the brothers would soon be together.

*****

By the middle of August, they had

constructed three small cabins in the middle of the property, and they had a growing herd of cattle. Walton had noticed an advertisement in the local paper for mail order brides. He knew Bart had no intention of marrying, and Nate wanted to wait until the ranch was more stable, but they were younger than him, after all. By the time their brides arrived, they'd understand his need to have a family.

After their supper of beans and beans that evening, Walton's brothers went home and left him alone as they did every night. He sat at his small table and wrote a letter.

Dear Miss Miller,

My brothers and I have a large ranch about an hour out of Wiggieville, Texas. We've built three houses here and have the start of a good herd of cattle. That means we're ready to marry. We're identical triplets, so we're all about six foot with brown hair and brown eyes. We're strong men and perfectly capable of providing for brides and any little ones that may come along.

We're twenty-seven, and would really like women between the ages of eighteen and twenty-six. Looks aren't terribly important, but they need to be willing to work hard and cook well. We're all sick of eating our own cooking.

I look forward to your response.

Sincerely,

Walton, Nate and Bart Dalton

Walton folded the letter and set it aside. He'd mail it when he went to town for supplies the next morning. Soon, they'd have women doing their cooking and cleaning. Not to mention keeping them warm at night.

Walton smiled. He liked the idea of a little lady to keep him warm at night more than he was willing to express.

The Sisters

Gwen Blue hurried through the dark streets of Beckham. Why had Gertie wanted to meet her so late at night? She was going to be married to Stanley in just a couple of weeks, so she wasn't certain why the woman would want to meet her most bitter enemy at all, but she'd go. The letter had said something about mending fences, which sounded good to Gwen after a lifetime of hateful rivalry.

When she arrived at the schoolhouse where they had once been classmates, she looked around. She'd always loved this playground, but it seemed different at night. It was scary.

Stanley stepped around the schoolhouse

and walked to her. "Oh, Gwen, I'm so glad you've come!"

Gwen looked at her old suitor with surprise. "What are you doing here?" Stanley stepped closer to her, and Gwen took a step back. "I was supposed to be meeting Gertie."

Stanley reached out and touched her cheek. "I wrote that letter, Gwen. I can't marry Gertie when I'm still in love with you. I never should have broken off our courtship. Will you forgive me and give me another chance?"

Gwen stared at him in disbelief before finally shaking her head. "First, let's get one thing straight. You did not break off our courtship. I did. I broke it off when I saw you looking at Gertie's bosom after church one day. Second, you brought me here under false pretenses? No, I will not forgive you. No, I will not take you back. You need to marry

Gertie like you promised. If you don't, everyone will always know what a cad you are. Don't contact me again."

Gwen was practically shaking with anger as she spun on her heel to go back home. She'd thought she and Gertie would be able to put their past behind them. No, it was just Stanley being selfish once again.

Stanley put his hand on Gwen's shoulder and spun her back around. "You know you still love me!"

He crushed his lips to hers, and she stomped on his foot to get him to release her. How had she ever thought she loved this man? "Let go of me, you fool!" She tore away from him and rushed away. She never should have come.

*****

Two days later at church, Gwen sat with

her sisters, Bonnie and Libby, wondering why the ladies of the church refused to speak to her on her way to the pew. Some even moved their dresses out of the way to keep them from touching her. She felt like a pariah, and she didn't even know what she'd done to be treated that way.

Bonnie and Libby had received the same treatment for the most part, but no one had avoided getting touched by them. Gwen had always been the most popular girl in their entire congregation, with men flocking around her, but that had changed as well. Even her current sweetheart, Norbert Rumfield, had refused to speak to her. She didn't know what people thought she'd done, but she certainly hadn't. Whatever it was.

Their mother took her seat on the other side of Bonnie, and leaned over glaring at Gwen. "Why do all my friends think you're pregnant?"

Gwen stared back at her mother, her mind spinning. Pregnant? Yes, she'd probably kissed a few more boys than she should have over the years, but she'd never even let one of them touch her breast. No, she wasn't pregnant. Who would say that?

"I have no idea, Mama. I'm not. I swear!"

Bonnie and Libby snickered. They loved it when Gwen was in trouble. She always shamed them because she was always kissing all the boys. There weren't enough men in town when Gwen was around.

Sarah Blue looked back and forth between her oldest and youngest daughters. "What are you two laughing about? Rumors also say the two of you were seen kissing the same boy! Where did I go wrong?"

Bonnie and Libby exchanged glances. "Never!" Bonnie exclaimed. "I've never even kissed one man, Mama."

Libby shook her head. "Gwen always beats us to the boys. We never get a chance to kiss them."

Gwen glared at Libby. "I can't believe you just said that! I hate you!" She stood up and ran out of the church. People were saying mcan horrible things about hcr, and shc wasn't about to put up with it.

When she got outside, she wiped away her tears. Leaning against the back of the church, she sighed. Why were people always willing to believe bad things about her? No, she wasn't an angel and never pretended to be. But she wasn't a whore, and that's what people were making her out to be, and it just wasn't fair.

She did just as much volunteer work as the next woman and worked hard to make certain she always looked her best. It wasn't like she was shallow, she just felt like the orphans in town deserved to see a pretty woman and not one with her hair all down around her shoulders looking scraggly.

She sat there for a minute before she realized her nemesis from her schooldays, Gertie Landry, was glaring at her. "I heard you kissed my beau in the park late one night this week," she sneered. "He's still marrying me, though."

Gwen looked at Gertie. Had she started the rumors? "I didn't kiss him. He forced a kiss on me. I told him I'm not interested in renewing our relationship. That's what he wants, you know. He wants me to take him back so he won't have to marry you."

Gwen knew her words were mean, but there were times when she just couldn't hold back, and just looking at Gertie had made her angry for years. Ever since the other girl had pushed her in the mud when she was on her way to her first church social. She hadn't been able to clean up enough, and Gertie had danced with her beau. Spiteful girl.

Gertie walked closer. "That's not true! He told me what happened. You saw him and ran to him in the park, demanding he break off our engagement, and then you flung your arms around his neck and kissed him. You're a tramp, Gwen Blue!"

"Did you start the rumors about me being pregnant?" Gwen stood up and faced the other girl.

"Now you won't be able to entice all the men you meet." Gertie smirked at Gwen.

"People are going to know you lied."

"By then I'll be happily married. Besides, I'll tell them you lost the baby. No big deal."

Gwen felt a growl rising in her throat. Never in her life had she wanted to hit anyone as much as she wanted to hit Gertie at that moment. She knew it was the wrong thing to do, but she just couldn't help herself. She balled up her fist, just like her brothers had taught her, and she punched Gertie right in the eye.

Gertie let out a loud wail, her hand covering her eye. Gwen stood there, knowing people would come to see what the ruckus was about. She planned to tell everyone right there and then that she had done nothing wrong.

When Mr. Blue saw Gwen standing over Gertie who was sprawled in the dirt, he didn't hesitate. He grabbed her by her ear and pulled her home. Her mother and sisters had come out of the church to see what happened and they followed along behind them. Their three brothers would have to represent the family in church that morning.

*****

When they got back to the house, their mother sat them all down in the parlor. "I want to know what on earth is going on with you! All of you!"

Gwen crossed her arms over her chest. "Gertie admitted that she started the rumors. I know it's not ladylike to hit someone, but sometimes I think that justice is more important than being ladylike."

Mrs. Blue looked at Gwen and shook her head. "I have to disagree, if you're hitting someone on church grounds during Sunday morning service! What were you thinking?"

Mr. Blue glared at his wife. "She's obviously thinking that you're going to let her get away with whatever she does like you always have. You have turned all three girls into little snobs. Gwen runs around with a different man every other week. We heard she was in trouble, and we both believed it! That tells me there's a problem right there. No more. I'm going to find husbands for all three of them."

Gwen jumped out of her chair. She'd always been the most vocal of the three. "I won't do it! You can't make me marry someone I don't want to marry! What are you going to do? Lock me in my room?"

Mr. Blue's face turned red with anger. "That's exactly what I'm going to do. You have been out of control for too long. From now on you will take all of your meals in your room. You may come out to use the water closet, but only if your mother or I accompany you." He grabbed her by her upper arm and dragged her up the stairs to her small room.

Gwen threw herself on her bed and sobbed loudly, knowing her mother would never hold out against her sobs. She never had, and she never would.

*****

Libby and Bonnie sat in the parlor with their mother listening to Gwen's wails. "Mama, you can't really let Papa lock Gwen up until she marries," insisted Libby. "Can you?"

Mrs. Blue shrugged. "I have no control over him. He's my husband. I was taught to honor and obey my parents *and* my husband. I should have taught you three girls to do the same thing." She shook her head. "I'm afraid I'll have to let your papa do whatever he thinks is right this time."

Libby and Bonnie exchanged a look.

"Would it be all right if we went in to talk to her?" Bonnie asked. She had an idea, one that she'd been formulating for a while, and she needed to talk to her sisters about it.

Mrs. Blue eyed her eldest daughter for a moment before shaking her head. "I don't think that's a good idea. I don't trust you girls not to let her out."

"But…you can't think to keep us apart for as long as it takes to plan a wedding! That's ridiculous." Libby couldn't believe her mother would even think of doing such a thing.

Bonnie reached over and squeezed Libby's hand, her way of signaling that she had an idea.

Mrs. Blue sighed. "I don't know what we'll do. I just know I'm not going to fight with my husband about the punishment you girls have been given. I'm done protecting you from him. After today, I'm done helping you at all. You all shamed me today."

Libby shook her head. "No, Mama. Only Gwen shamed you. We were good."

Mrs. Blue was startled by that for a moment. "Oh, you were. It was only Gwen, wasn't it?"

"I think we'll go up to our room now." Bonnie got to her feet and looked at Libby, letting her know without a word that they had some serious talking to do.

Gwen had always had her own room because she was too bossy to share with her sisters. They liked their room more orderly than she did, and her response was always, "Clean up my stuff yourself then." It worked out better for everyone.

As soon as they reached their room, Bonnie closed the door. She got something out of her dresser drawer and sat down on the bed. Once Libby was sitting in front of her, she handed her the letter she'd gotten.

Libby looked down at the letter. "What's this?"

Bonnie shrugged. "Libby, we both know I have no future in Beckham. Next to you and Gwen, I'm the ugly duckling. Goodness, everyone calls me 'Scrawny Bonnie' behind my back, don't pretend they don't. I've never had a single suitor, while you both have had plenty of men interested in you — and I'm the oldest! I'm twenty-three and an old maid."

Libby started to protest but Bonnie interrupted her. "I've come to terms with it, Libby. But that doesn't mean I don't want to marry. Unlike you and Gwen, though, I don't subscribe to the fantasy that I will only marry for love. A business arrangement would suit me just fine, so I spoke to Elizabeth Miller, the lady who runs the mail order bride agency."

Libby gasped at that. "Did you get a proposal? Are you leaving us?!"

"Read the letter," Bonnie murmured.

Libby read it and looked up and her sister, confused. "But this letter is looking for three women, not one."

Bonnie nodded. "I was going to talk to a couple of other unattached friends my age but... Libby, we need to leave town as soon as possible. Did you see the look in Papa's eyes? He's really going to marry us off, and I suspect it's to that trio of creepy old deacons from church he's been speaking with every Sunday. I couldn't stand that humiliation.

"No! Not them! He wouldn't dare! I'm only eighteen! Mother wouldn't let him."

"Didn't you hear her? She won't protect you and Gwen anymore, Libby. I know that's hard to hear since she's spoiled you two so much, but I can tell you from experience, that when she gives up on you, it's forever."

Libby had a pained look on her face as if she was trying to figure out a puzzle. Bonnie knew to just wait. Sometimes it took her beautiful sister a little bit longer to catch on, but she always did...eventually.

"So instead of marrying those old lechers, we run away to Texas and marry strangers?"

"At least they're young strangers, Libby. We can start completely from scratch without anyone knowing about this ridiculous scandal. Even if Papa doesn't force us to marry his friends, no one else will want us for a very long time, if ever."

Libby gave Bonnie a sly look. "Do we have to take Gwen?"

Bonnie smiled. "She may be annoying, but she's our sister. She probably needs this more than either of us. Let's rescue her from herself, Libby. What do you say?"

After a moment Libby nodded. "Let's make it happen."

Chapter One

Gwen Blue laid in her bed, staring at the wall. She'd been locked in her room for eight weeks, and she no longer cared about anything. She hadn't bathed in over a month. She barely ate the food her mother brought her. Maybe if she starved herself enough, her groom would take one look at her and refuse to marry her. Maybe if she smelled bad enough, he would simply walk away. She had no other way of fighting back!

When her parents had first locked her in her room, she'd been certain she could charm her way out as she always had. Sure, her mother never said anything she didn't mean, but Papa? He was usually a pushover.

She had only seen him once since she'd

been locked away, though. She shuddered as she thought of the evening he'd come into her room.

"Well, I've found a solution for you, Gwen. You and your sisters are going to marry the three deacons from church. You have been blessed to be selected by Deacon Bellafonte. The marriage will take place in one month. That will give you enough time that everyone will know you're not marrying him because you're with child." Mr. Blue's words were spoken in an excited voice, as if he thought he was bestowing a gift on his middle daughter.

Gwen stared at her father in open mouthed astonishment. "Deacon Bellafonte? He's old! And he smells bad! Worse, he's a lecher. He tries to get all the young ladies alone. I can't marry him, Papa. You know I can't!" Why would anyone think he was an appropriate husband for a twenty-one year old girl?

Mr. Blue's jaw hardened. "You've left me with no other option. You acted like a loose woman, and it's up to me to protect the family's name and reputation. You'll do what you're told." He left the room after that, his eyes not softening one bit.

Gwen had picked up a pitcher and threw it at the door, screaming at the top of her lungs. "I can't marry him! You can't make me!"

She hadn't left the room since. A chamber pot had been brought in for her personal use, and there had been no baths brought to her. Good thing, because she would have refused to use a tub, just as she'd refused the pitcher and bowl. No, she wasn't about to keep clean when being disgusting could possibly cause Deacon Bellafonte to move on.

She shuddered thinking about him. He

was a scrawny old man with dark hair and teeth that were all but black. He must be at least forty-five! No, she wouldn't marry him. If she had to tell the man he repulsed her, she would happily do so.

She rolled over in her bed and felt the silent tears falling again. Before 'the incident' she'd only ever cried when she needed something from someone. She'd always been able to cry on command. Now? The tears were real, and they weren't pretty.

She'd just drifted off to sleep when she felt someone's hand on her. She jerked, imagining it was Deacon Bellafonte. She'd taken to having nightmares about his hands on her body. She rubbed her eyes quickly looking around her. Where was she?

"Gwenny, wake up. Gwen, can you hear me?" Bonnie was leaning over her in her bed.

Gwen almost sagged with relief as she realized it was her older sister and not her intended. She said the most intelligent thing that came to mind. "Muh?"

"Gwen, do you want to marry old man Bellafonte?"

"No!" How could Bonnie even ask her that? Did Gwen's sister not know her at all?

"Shhh! You can't make any noise, understand? If you don't want marry him, we need to leave tonight." Bonnie kept her voice low, obviously trying to keep their parents from waking.

Gwen was willing to do anything to get away from her marriage, but fear of the unknown was strong. She knew she couldn't make a living. She had no real skills like Bonnie did. "But where will we go?"

"To visit my old school friend, Anna Simpson, in Texas. We already have tickets and we've packed as much as we dare because no one in the family knows. If we wake them up, they'll stop us and we'll be forced to marry those old men."

Just then Hank hurried in with the coat. Gwen gasped and scrambled backward. "No!" She couldn't trust Hank to help her and her sisters. She couldn't trust anyone!

"Darling, Hank is helping us," Bonnie whispered. "He's the only one, and he's promised to keep our secret until his death." She turned to give her brother a withering look. "Which will come quickly if he betrays us."

Hank simply nodded and wrapped her coat around her shoulders. Gwen wanted to shy away from him, but after two months of inactivity, she had little strength.

"Let's go, Gwenny."

"But…look at me," she said quietly. How

could anyone think she could leave town in such a state? She glanced in the mirror by the little bit of light drifting in the window from the moon. Her usually perfectly coiffed blond hair hung in greasy clumps around her face. She could see that she'd lost weight. For the first time in weeks, her looks mattered again.

"I have a plan, but we have to leave now."

Gwen studied her sister for a moment before nodding. "All right. I'll trust you."

The four of them crept from the house, Hank driving them to a house Gwen had seen but never been in. She knew it had once been the home of wealthy but eccentric Harriett Long, but now a young woman who had been raised just outside of town lived there. She couldn't think of the woman's name.

Bonnie jumped down from the buckboard. "Hank, take the trunk to the train station.

We'll be there soon. Then take the buckboard home and pretend you know nothing of this. You don't need Papa angry with you, too."

Gwen watched as Bonnie hugged Hank, kissing his cheek.

Hank nodded. "I'll do it. Be careful." He reached out a hand as if to touch Gwen, but let it drop away.

Gwen was so filthy, even her own brother wouldn't touch her, and Bonnie wanted her to go to the most elegant home in all of Beckham? What was she thinking?

Bonnie marched straight to the door and pounded on it as if they had every right in the world to be there. What had her sister been up to while she was locked away?

It took five minutes and a lot of pounding, but finally a young blond head poked out the door. "Ladies, come in. What's the trouble? Oh!" The woman took a long look at Gwen.

Gwen blushed. No one had ever seen her looking so bad. She had never in her life dreamed she'd allow herself to look this way. She kept quiet, too embarrassed to speak.

"Our train leaves in about three hours, Elizabeth. We need your help." Bonnie shoved Gwen at Elizabeth.

Elizabeth nodded and led them into the house, taking the sisters to a small bathroom. "You can clean up in there." She pointed to the bathroom. "Do you have clean clothes for her?" Elizabeth asked.

Bonnie nodded. "We do. These are my sisters as I'm sure you've guessed. The clean one is Libby. The rancid one is Gwen."

Gwen glared at Bonnie but didn't say a word. How could she? She *was* rancid.

Gwen hurriedly bathed, soaping and rinsing her hair three times. She felt disgusting. It was as if she'd just woken from a horrible nightmare. Her mind was suddenly working again. She needed to be clean!

The entire time she was bathing, she could hear soft voices from another room. She decided she didn't care if they were talking about her. She wasn't going to marry that horrible monster, and she was getting clean. Everything would be all better soon.

When she was finished, she took the clothes Libby had left for her and dressed quickly. Why hadn't they brought her cornflower blue dress? Yes, she knew she looked good in the yellow one too, but the cornflower matched her eyes better and would show off her tiny waist, which was even smaller now that she'd lost weight.

She did her best to get her curls just perfect before opening the door and wandering until she found the others in a large office. Elizabeth sat, still in her dressing gown, at a small desk while Libby and Bonnie sat on a sofa. Holding her hand out to meet Elizabeth officially, she said, "I'm Gwen Blue." As she said the words, she realized she could hold her head up again. All of her confidence was back now that she was no longer filthy.

Elizabeth smiled. "It's nice to meet you, Gwen."

"You as well." Gwen looked around the beautiful home and knew she needed to live somewhere like that someday soon. She deserved the nicest things in life. She knew, because her papa had always told her she did. The only good thing about old man Bellafonte was his wealth. She shuddered as she thought of him. She'd even marry a poor man to escape Mr. Bellafonte.

Bonnie got to her feet. "We'd better be off to the train station. Thank you so much for your help."

As they were leaving the house, Gwen decided to ask the main thing she needed to know. Anyone else would have asked how the sisters knew Elizabeth, but not Gwen. There was something a great deal more important to her. "Libby, why didn't you bring my cornflower dress?"

Libby looked disgusted. "I see you're back to normal again," she hissed.

"What was that?" Gwen couldn't believe her sister would say that! It was a legitimate question. She wanted her prettiest dress. Was that too much to ask?

"I said—"

"We need to let Elizabeth get back to sleep and get ourselves to the train before it leaves us to a horrible fate," Bonnie interrupted, obviously annoyed the two of them were starting to bicker in front of the other woman.

As they were rushing toward the street, Elizabeth called out, "Now you three have a safe journey, and be sure to write to tell me how everything is going with those three brothers!"

Bonnie waved, but Libby remained silent.

"Brothers? What brothers?" Gwen asked. Something strange was going on, and she wanted to know what it was.

"Our brothers, silly," Bonnie replied. "Now get moving or we'll miss the train." She exchanged a look with Libby.

Gwen shook her head. Let them keep their silly secrets. She was clean and off on an adventure. And the best part of it all was she didn't have to marry Deacon Bellafonte. She'd been saved from her worst nightmare by the unlikeliest of heroines. Her sister, Bonnie.

*****

The trip to Texas took ten days, and after the first twenty-four hours, Gwen remembered why she didn't particularly like her sisters. Oh, she loved them, but she didn't always like them.

Bonnie, well, Bonnie was the oldest and the smartest. She was the best at absolutely everything. She could sew, quilt, cook, knit, crochet, and even tat better than anyone Gwen had ever seen. She could also do sums in her head at an incredible speed. She never misspoke. Her grammar was impeccable.

In short, Bonnie was perfect in every way but one. She wasn't beautiful. That was Gwen's role. Gwen had never needed to be smart or good at anything. She just needed to be pretty and smile a lot, and she'd get her way. It had always been that way for them.

Libby was the youngest of the three, but she was also the one with the sweetest expression. You could look at Libby and believe her perfect in every way. She wasn't, though. She was pretty, not nearly as beautiful as Gwen, of course, but she was only eighteen, and hadn't really rounded out everywhere yet. No, it was her personality that Gwen wasn't fond of.

Libby complained that Gwen thought too much of her looks, but in reality, Libby was the one obsessed with beauty. Gwen just had to be clean to be beautiful, while Libby had to work at it. So work at it, she did. She spent hours every day fussing with her hair and pinching her cheeks to bring them color. She wanted lip rouge and tried her best to cajole their mother into buying her some, but when she refused, she'd taken to smearing berry juice on her lips to keep them rosy.

Gwen rolled her eyes at Libby. "Why are you always fussing with your hair? We have to be on this train for another five days. We've seen every man there is to see. Why bother?"

Libby glared at Gwen. "Some of us care about how we look."

"Some of us don't have to," Gwen returned, knowing she was being snotty. Libby brought out the worst in her, though. She loved her younger sister with all her heart, but sometimes, she just wanted to hit her.

"Would you two stop it?" Bonnie asked. "You're making me crazy! I want to finish this apron today so that I can give it to Anna as a gift for inviting us."

"What's going on with us visiting Anna? You two were never really that close, were you? I mean, I know she was the only real friend you had, but it's not like you ever spent a lot of time together outside of school."

Bonnie shook her head. "We've kept up a correspondence. I like Anna a lot. When she heard about our situation, she suggested we come out there. I'm hoping we'll meet some men while we're there. Texas doesn't have enough women, you know."

Gwen smiled. She loved men. She'd never done the things she'd been accused of, but she loved them. There just wasn't enough time to court them all. She had a bad reputation in Beckham because she'd stepped out with so many men. She hadn't done more than kiss any of them, though.

And the incident? Why, she hadn't been doing anything wrong at all. She'd met with an old beau because he'd tricked her. When he grabbed her and kissed her, she'd been stunned. She hadn't asked for his affections.

He was engaged to Gertrude, the second prettiest girl in Beckham, who hated Gwen, who was the prettiest girl in Beckham.

Gertie had then spread rumors that Gwen was with child and that she, Bonnie, and Libby had all been seen kissing the same man. As if any man had ever kissed Bonnie!

The lies had been bad for her reputation, but they'd been great for Bonnie's. I mean, what man wanted to court a woman that no other man had even looked twice at?

A man came around with a tray of food and she got a sandwich. She ignored her sisters as she stared out the window eating it. There were men in Texas. More men than women. Texas sounded like paradise.

*****

On the last day of the trip, Gwen did her

best to wash her hands and face with the water provided for the passengers to drink. She knew that wasn't what she was supposed to do with it, but really? They were almost to Weatherford, where they would take a stagecoach to a place called Wiggieville.

What kind of name was Wiggieville anyway? Honestly, Gwen didn't care where they were going as long as they were ending up somewhere she didn't have to marry an old man, and where she could find a man to court her. Or several men. Gwen wasn't certain she was ready to marry, but courting certainly was fun.

Just before the train pulled into the station, Gwen sat up straight, more excited than she could express. Bonnie and Libby looked nervous. Bonnie was practically green. "Is the motion starting to make you sick, Bonnie?"

Bonnie shook her head slowly. "I'm just nervous. I've never had to take a stagecoach before."

"You weren't nervous before we took the train, and you've never taken a train before. How could you be nervous about taking a stagecoach? You're just being silly." Sometimes Gwen didn't understand her sisters at all.

Bonnie nodded slowly. "I probably am."

Libby sighed. "I hope mine's handsome."

Gwen eyed Libby suspiciously. "You hope your *what* is handsome?"

Bonnie elbowed Libby. "She hopes the man she eventually meets and marries is handsome, of course. We're all hoping to find a good handsome man here in Texas, aren't we?"

Gwen looked back and forth between her sisters. There was something they weren't telling her. Every time she went to the back of their car to relieve herself when she came back, her sisters were deep in conversation.

Oh well, whatever they were up to didn't have anything to do with her. They both knew better than to try to get her to do anything she didn't want to do. They'd seen the fit she'd thrown when Papa said she had to marry Deacon Bellafonte. They wouldn't try to force her to do anything.

She watched out the window as the train came to a stop. "It's...flat. And dry. Why is all the grass brown here?"

Bonnie answered her quickly. "From what I've read, there are frequent droughts in Texas. There's not enough rainfall, so often by this time of year, the grass is brown and withered."

Gwen wrinkled her nose. "Well, that doesn't sound pleasant. I was thinking I'd find a man here and stay, but maybe I'll move on." She knew there was no way she could move on without her sisters, but she didn't care. It felt like she was in a new world with a new life and new possibilities. She could talk about moving on if she wanted to.

Bonnie and Libby exchanged another one of their knowing looks with each other. Gwen had just about had it. "What are you two keeping from me? You obviously have a secret, and I want to know what it is!"

Bonnie sighed. "I guess it's time we told you anyway. Gwen--"

"Weatherford station!" the conductor called out as the train came to a stop.

Gwen bounced out of her seat, completely forgetting her sister was about to tell her something. They were finally going to get off this confounded train! In ten days they'd had three hours without the world moving under them, and that was just when they'd changed trains in St. Louis. She jumped into the aisle and took Libby's hand, pulling her to her feet. "Let's get off this train!"

Bonnie bit her lip, but she stood, getting into the aisle at the center of the train with her sisters.

Chapter Two

Gwen rushed off the train and immediately started looking around for the stagecoach. Bonnie caught up to her, putting her hand on her sister's shoulder. "Don't run off now!"

"I'm looking for the stagecoach. It's only another three hours, and we'll be there. I can't wait to see Anna." Really, it wasn't so much seeing Anna that she cared about. She needed to be in one place for a while. The journey had been much too long for her.

"You didn't even like Anna," Bonnie argued.

"Well, I love her today, because she's going to let me sleep in a bed that doesn't move!" Gwen looked at Bonnie. "The bed *won't* move will it? She doesn't live on a boat or something silly like that?"

Bonnie laughed. "No, I don't think the bed will move." She led the way to the platform. "We need to wait for our trunk to be unloaded."

Gwen laughed. "I was so excited to be on the stagecoach, I forgot all about my trunk. That was silly of me, wasn't it?"

Libby and Bonnie exchanged looks. "Our trunk, Gwenny. We could only pack one trunk for the three of us or Mama and Papa would have gotten suspicious."

"Are you serious? You'd better have packed my cornflower blue dress. It's my favorite." Gwen looked between her sisters.

Bonnie sighed. "We couldn't. We didn't have access to your clothes at all, because you were locked in your room, remember? We brought some of Libby's dresses for you."

Gwen made a face. "Libby's dresses? But Libby and I don't look good in the same colors. I'm blond, and Libby's a brunette." Besides, she wanted her own clothes. Clothes that had been made just for her.

"I'll make you a new cornflower blue dress, Gwen. I promise. Just...don't make a fuss."

Gwen looked at her sister, surprised by her words. "A fuss? Why would I make a fuss?" She could see by Bonnie's face something was still wrong. "What were you going to tell me?"

Bonnie sighed. "Well, we're not exactly here to see Anna."

Gwen raised an eyebrow, more than a little annoyed her sisters had lied to her. "Why are we here then?"

"I..." Bonnie avoided Gwen's gaze, something she'd never done.

It must be bad, Gwen thought. *If Bonnie can't tell me what's going on, she's done something terrible.*

At that moment two men, who were obviously twin brothers, stepped between them. "Are you ladies the Blue sisters?" one of them asked. He had brown eyes and black hair. His shoulders were the broadest she'd ever seen. She wouldn't mind stepping out with him at all.

Gwen nodded slowly. "Who are you?" She'd never seen these men in her life. Why were they looking for them? Were they there to drive them to their new home, wherever it may be? She still didn't know *why* they were in Texas.

The man who'd asked the question grinned. "I'm Walton Dalton, and I pick you." He grabbed her hand and pulled her into his arms before she had a chance to reply. His mouth covered hers and he kissed her, right there in the middle of the train station.

Gwen stomped on his foot, enjoying the kiss, but she knew it wasn't proper to kiss a man she'd just met. "Unhand me!" She wiped her hand across her mouth, trying to stop the tingling that had started as soon as his lips had met hers.

Walt smiled down at Gwen. "I'll unhand you for now. Preacher's standing by." He kept his arm firmly around his little fiancé's shoulders. "Which sister are you?"

"I'm Gwendolyn. Why do you persist in touching me? I don't know you!" She struggled against him, but realized it was futile. He was much stronger than she would ever be.

Bonnie smiled at Walt. "I'm Bonnie. I'm the oldest sister. I believe I'm the one you're supposed to marry."

Walt looked back and forth between the sisters. "I don't care who's oldest. I'm marrying this one." He nodded at Nate. "That's my brother Nate. Bart should be here by now, but I'm sure he'll be along." He'd better be along. He'd promised Walt he'd be there by three. It was quarter after.

Bonnie glared at Walt and turned to Nate, who was openly staring at Libby. "Libby's the youngest," she announced, seeming to think that would matter to the brothers.

Nate looked back and forth between Walt and Bonnie. "I thought we were here to see a man about some cattle."

Walt grinned at his brother. "Surprise! Since Bart isn't here, you get next pick. Which one do you want for your bride?" He didn't expect a lot of problems from Nate. Bart was the one who would protest the loudest.

Nate blinked. "You sent off for brides for us? The cattle salesman was a lie?"

Walt shrugged. "I didn't think you'd come if I told you why we were really here." He kissed the top of Gwen's head as if they'd been in love for years. "Pick one." He wasn't letting this little beauty go. He'd expected all three sisters to be homely. Gwen had been a fabulous surprise.

Nate pointed at Libby. "I guess I'll take the youngest." He leaned close to Walt and whispered, "I'll take care of *you* later."

Gwen gasped in shock. "You can't just pick me and say you'll marry me. No! What on earth is happening here? Bonnie? What have you done?" As grateful as Gwen was to her sister for rescuing her, she was furious about this arrangement. She had no desire to marry a stranger or anyone else for that matter.

Bonnie blinked as if fighting tears. "Libby knew why we were here. We just didn't want you to be stubborn. We rescued you after all."

"Rescued me? You kept me from marrying a crazy old man, yes, but he was at least someone I knew! Now you expect me to marry a total stranger? He has a stupid name! I can't marry a man named Walton Dalton! Who would name their child that? What if he thinks we should name our child Dalton Dalton or something?"

Walton flushed under his tan. "You're my bride. You have no right to be making fun of my name like that. My pa's name was Alton, and he wanted to have another special name like that for me." What right did she think she had to make fun of his name?

Gwen turned on him, inexplicably angry with the stranger. "Special? You think your name is special? Well, let me tell you, it's not. It's just plain silly. I can't marry a man who has such an awful name. Find someone else."

Walt put his hands on each of her shoulders and leaned down until they were on eye level with one another. "I've found my bride. We're marrying today. Don't make me take you over my knee as soon as we get home."

"You're threatening to spank me? Really? Because I'm not just falling in line to marry you? I thought I was coming here to visit an old school friend. I had no idea the real reason I was here was to marry a stranger. You can't blame me for getting angry about that."

Walt shrugged. "Maybe I can't get angry for that, but I can certainly be mad at you for the way you're talking to me. I didn't trick you. Your sister did. Take it out on her."

Gwen glared at everyone. "I'll be back." She turned on her heel and headed for the outhouse she'd seen at the back of the train station.

She was halfway there when she realized she was being followed. She spun around. "What exactly do you want now? I'm afraid I need to relieve myself, and you're not exactly welcome to help me do that."

Walt nodded. "I can understand that, ma'am." He stood looking at her, saying nothing else.

Gwen wanted to kick him, but she turned around again and went to the outhouse, flinging the door open and slamming it in his face. She'd never met such a hardheaded, handsome man in her life.

She sighed. She really didn't even need to relieve herself. She just needed some time away from him. She closed her eyes and thought about her options. She had no money. She knew no one except Anna, who was another three hours away by stagecoach. A stagecoach she couldn't afford to pay for.

Did she really have a choice? Could she not marry the stranger? Maybe there was a job she could find. A place she could go to meet people who might want to hire her. Of course, she had no real skills other than flirting and looking pretty, but maybe someone would want her.

She sighed. Truly she knew better. There were no jobs for women who didn't know how to do anything. None. No, she was going to have to marry the man. Walton Dalton indeed.

She stepped out of the outhouse finally to see Walton standing a few feet away with his back to her. Why had he waited that whole time? "Why are you still here?"

Walt turned to her. "I couldn't leave you here alone unprotected, ma'am." He tipped his hat to her. "Even if you don't want to marry me, it's my job to keep you safe until you decide what you do want to do."

Gwen sighed. "I'll marry you." Her voice was a mere mumble.

"What was that?"

"I'll marry you. There's really no other logical solution." She shrugged and started back toward the others.

"No."

"No?" she asked. What did he mean by 'no?'

"That's not what you do when you agree to marry someone. When you get engaged, you let your man kiss you. Let me demonstrate." He looked around. They were back behind the train station, which had been bustling mere moments before but now was relatively quiet. He caught her hand and pulled her to him until their chests were pressing together.

As his head lowered toward hers, she noticed his brown eyes and was struck again by how handsome he was. Even with all the men she'd stepped out with in Beckham, this man was the best looking of them all. She pressed her lips against his, knowing that she was going to marry him. Besides, she liked kissing.

As soon as their lips met, Walt took control of the kiss. He put his hands at her waist and kissed her for all he was worth. This little spitfire was exactly what he'd been needing. She made his blood boil, with both anger and passion. He couldn't believe how lucky he was.

When they broke the kiss, both of them

were out of breath. "We're marrying today."

Gwen raised a brow. "Today? Isn't it a little late in the day for that?" He wasn't going to give her time to get used to the idea? To make a pretty new dress for the occasion?

"Preacher's standing by. We just need to wait for Bart."

"Is Bart going to marry Bonnie?" Suddenly she worried about her older sister. The other two had been quick to reject her. Would their brother Bart do the same thing?

Walt shrugged. "He's going to have to. He just doesn't know it yet."

*****

They rejoined the others, Walt constantly giving Gwen amorous looks. She'd never been openly stared at the way Walt was staring at her, and it made her uncomfortable, but there was more to it than that.

By the time Bart finally arrived, she couldn't force herself to pay attention to the conversation, but instead she continued to watch as Walt dealt with his younger brother. She didn't care at all about Bart, though. If he made Bonnie unhappy, well then it was her own fault. She was the one who had decided to force them all to leave home and marry anyway, wasn't she? Even as she thought the words, she felt a pang for her sister. Poor Bonnie.

Less than two hours after they got off the train, they walked through town to the preacher's house. Gwen was nervous, but she wasn't going to let that stop her. She had to marry or she'd have nowhere to go. She could do it. She knew she could.

She couldn't remember anything of the ceremony later until the pastor said, "You may now kiss your brides." She'd never forget what happened then.

Walt took her into his arms and pulled her against him, kissing her as if he had every right in the world to hold her and never let her go. She shuddered as he straightened. Her sisters were both glaring at her as she stood there blushing. Why were they angry with her? She'd only done what they wanted her to do and married the man, right?

Walt and Nate had brought their own wagons, and she ignored her sisters as Walt helped her into his. She wanted to hug her sisters goodbye not knowing when she'd see them again, but she couldn't force herself to do it. They'd deceived her and brought her to the middle of Texas of all places. For a visit was fine. To dream about marrying a handsome cowboy was fine. To force her to marry a man she didn't know at all? That wasn't fine. She wasn't certain she'd ever speak with either of them again.

The last she saw of them was Bonnie crawling into the back of Nate's wagon while Libby sat on the seat beside her new husband. Bart was riding along beside them on his horse.

Walt drove in silence, his eyes on the road. They were ten minutes out of town before she couldn't stand it another minute. "Will I ever see my sisters again?"

Walt laughed. "We set up the ranch so that the three houses were each on our separate parcels of land, but they're only about a hundred yards apart in a triangle. We wanted to be able to go back and forth easily." Poor girl had thought she'd never see her sisters again. He knew his bond with his brothers was closer than most brothers, but he couldn't imagine spending the rest of his life without them.

Gwen closed her eyes with relief. She wouldn't be alone in a place where she knew no one after all. "That's good. I would miss my sisters," she said simply.

Walt understood exactly. She'd been deceived about coming to Texas, but she still loved her sisters. It was exactly how he felt about his brothers. Even though they made him crazy at times, he loved them with everything inside him. How could he not? Looking at them was like looking into a mirror. "We'll see a lot of them, I'm sure. I wouldn't be surprised if you ladies got together every day while we men did the real work on the ranch." He tore his eyes from the road and looked at her. "Do you want me to make a list of my favorite foods so you know what to cook for me?"

Gwen gasped in shock. "You don't have

servants to do the cooking? I thought you owned a ranch." He didn't really expect her to do menial chores, did he? She didn't know how!

Walt blinked a couple of times. "I do own a ranch, but it's a ranch we just started earlier in the year." He laughed briefly. "You really thought you wouldn't have to do your own cooking and cleaning? You're in for a real surprise, little lady."

She shook her head. "I don't cook or clean. You married the wrong sister if you want someone who's good at domestic chores."

Walt sighed. "Well, whichever of your sisters is good at those things can teach you, I suppose. How hard can it be to learn?"

"Very hard if you have no desire to learn," she mumbled beneath her breath.

"What was that?"

"Oh, nothing."

"I'm sure you said something." Walton was beginning to realize that his bride was the spunky one. Maybe he should have taken the red head after all.

"If it had been meant for your ears, I'd have said it loudly enough for you to hear me." She stared at the vast fields of dry grass. "How far is it to the ranch?"

"Bout three hours from town. We won't make it before dark."

Three hours from the nearest town? Really? "Is there nowhere closer to buy supplies?" She thought of the dress her sister had promised to make for her. Would they even be able to find cornflower blue fabric here in this godforsaken place?

"There's a smaller town up the road apiece. You'll go there for supplies." He was glad she was thinking about the things they'd need. Even if she couldn't cook now, he was certain her sister could teach her.

When they finally reached the dirt road leading up to the cabins, he smiled. Every time he pulled onto his own land, it made him happy. He'd done a lot of things since he'd left home at the age of eighteen, but always he'd dreamed of having his own land. A place where he could raise a family. With the beautiful woman beside him, he could start that family.

He helped her down from the wagon and told her to go in without him while he took care of the horses.

Gwen stood in front of the tiny cabin, filled with shock. This was where she was expected to live? She felt a tear trickle down her face. Sure she was glad she didn't have to marry old man Bellafonte, but a hovel? In the middle of nowhere? What would she do for fun?

She walked into the house and was pleased to see that it wasn't filthy. Obviously he was a man who took pride in his surroundings. That would serve them both well. If he was already used to cleaning the house, he could just keep doing it. It would be no different than before, so shouldn't be a problem at all. It hadn't been her idea to marry him, so he really couldn't expect her to clean for him, could he?

By the moonlight streaming through the window, she found a lantern and lit it. The cabin was even smaller on the inside. Didn't he know he needed to be able to provide for a wife before he sent off for one?

She sat at the table and removed her gloves and bonnet. She was tired and hungry. She couldn't help but wonder what he planned to serve her for supper. Nothing was cooking, and she was very hungry.

Walt finished with the horses and wandered to the house, smiling to himself. He'd gotten a spirited little wife, and despite her lack of cooking skills, he was going to be happy.

When he stepped into the house, he found his little bride sitting at the table with her hands folded in front of her. She'd obviously done nothing other than light the lantern. "What's for supper?" he asked.

"I already told you, I don't know how to cook. What are you fixing for me?" She was hungry, and being hungry always made Gwen a bit testy. She tried to keep it from her voice, but she knew it had shone through.

"Well, there's no cooking involved with something simple like bread and butter. Or bread and jam. You could get that for us," he suggested politely. He wanted to order her to do it, but since he planned to bed her as soon as she'd finished the supper dishes, he was certain he should be a tad bit more polite about it than that.

"I've been traveling for ten days. I'm tired. I'm hungry. I want a bath. I think it's only fair that you take care of supper tonight while I rest." She stood and walked into the small bedroom that was sectioned off from the main area with a makeshift curtain.

Walt watched her go, shaking his head. He'd let her get away with her behavior just this once, because she was right. She had traveled for a long time, and she must be tired. Tomorrow, though. Tomorrow, she was going to fix supper for him, or by God, she'd have to deal with his anger.

Chapter Three

After supper, Gwen reluctantly washed the dishes. Walt had cooked, and it was the least she could do. After she finished, she turned to see him watching her, his eyes filled with lust. She knew the look, because she'd seen it so many times on the men she'd stepped out with. She knew what the look meant as well. It meant he'd do anything for her.

She smiled at Walton flirtatiously, sidling up to him. "The meal was lovely. I do appreciate you cooking for me." She really wanted a nice hot bath after all that time on trains. Surely he'd fetch water for her if she spoke sweetly enough.

Walt looked at her for a minute, knowing

she was up to something. It was time for him to assert his authority over her. He grabbed her by the waist and pulled her down onto his lap, one hand cupping her breast, while the other went behind her head to pull it down for a kiss.

Gwen had never had a man be so forward with her. No one had ever just grabbed her, other than that one time in the park with Stanley. She was used to men who asked permission before kissing her, not that she'd never been kissed against her will.

She melted into his kiss while her hand went to his and removed it from her breast. He had no right to touch her where no other man ever had. She put it on her waist, and then concentrated on kissing him back.

Walt almost chuckled at her puny attempts to thwart his advances. She was going to be under him in bed within the hour.

Why did she think she shouldn't let him touch her now?

His hand moved back to her breast while his other hand stroked up and down her back, soothing her.

Gwen was startled at his touch. Did she have to ask him not to touch her there? What was his problem?

Her hand once again went to the hand on her breast and put it back on her waist. She nipped at his bottom lip. This man certainly was a pleasure to kiss, unlike most of the men she'd stepped out with back in Beckham. They'd all made her feel like her skin was crawling when they'd touched their lips to hers.

Abruptly, Walt stood up and swung her into his arms, carrying her past the partition and to the bedroom, laying her gently on the bed.

Gwen propped herself up on her elbows. "I want a bath before bed." She'd kissed him, so surely he would do whatever she asked now. That's how it worked. That's how it had always worked.

Walt nodded. "You do smell a bit rank. Sure. The well is about a hundred yards behind the house. Fire's still going in the stove, so it shouldn't take too long to heat up."

She smiled. "Thank you for getting it ready for me." She knew she'd be able to wrap him around her finger with her kisses. Marriage wasn't going to be so bad after all.

He laughed. Did she really think he was going to fill her tub for her? Had the girl never done anything for herself in her life? He grabbed her hand and looked at the palm and fingertips. "Have you always had servants?"

"Yes, of course. Haven't you?"

He sighed. "Go to the well and get your water. I can wait." Not for long, but he could wait. She was going to be a joy in bed. He just hoped it made up for her spoiled attitude the rest of the time.

"Me? I thought you were going to carry the water in."

"No, ma'am. I'm not the one who wants a bath tonight." He eyed her for a moment. What was her name again? He knew Bonnie was the oldest, but she'd married Bart. Started with a G didn't it? Gertie?

"But it's hard work. I've never had to carry water into the house before. My family had running water." Gwen couldn't believe he was refusing to carry water for her. Hadn't she just let him kiss her?

"Well, I don't have running water, and you're going to need to get used to carrying your own water." He crossed his arms over his chest and stared down at her on the bed. She really did need a bath.

Gwen pushed up into a sitting position on the bed, glaring at him the whole while. "I don't want to carry the water." She stood up and walked toward him, trailing the tip of her finger down the middle of his chest. "Would you do it for me? Please?"

Walt had to stifle a laugh. Did she really think she was going to get around him that way? He'd seen women get men to do what they wanted by flirting before, but he'd never seen a married woman try it with her husband. And really? She was his to do with as he wanted. What difference did it make to him if she flirted with him? "I'll show you how."

He stepped away from her and led the way through the yard to the well. He carefully lowered the bucket and showed her how to do it, before taking it out and handing it to her. "You get this started boiling while I get the tub for you."

He usually just washed up at the basin, but a tin tub stood beside the house. He carried it into the kitchen and set it on the floor not far from the stove. He was finished before she even got into the house with the bucket.

Walt put a huge pot on the stove for her to heat the water in and sat down at the table, watching to see how she'd handle it.

Gwen couldn't believe he wouldn't heat the water for her. What kind of man would leave his own wife to carry water on her own? She was mumbling under her breath as she carried the bucket into the house and poured it into the pot on the stove. She looked at him. "How many more do I need?" She didn't want to talk to him ever again, but she had to. She should have just stayed on the train to the next stop. Surely there would have been a man there who knew how to treat a lady.

He shrugged. "Depends how full you want the water. I'd say at least ten hot and five cold."

She gaped at him openly. "And you expect me to carry it all myself?"

"I cooked dinner."

"Walton Dalton! What kind of man are you to expect me to do this kind of work when I've never done it before? Don't you think I need to learn to do this kind of hard work gradually? Do a little more each day?"

He sighed. She was probably right whether he liked it or not. "I'll help you. You stay here and boil the water, and I'll carry the buckets." He was annoyed with her. What kind of woman agreed to marry a rancher when she had no work skills? How was she ever going to adjust to ranch life?

He carried in bucket after bucket while she boiled the water and dumped it into his bathtub. He needed to make sure she knew he wasn't going to be doing this every day. She was a beautiful woman, but she couldn't use her beauty to get out of doing the work a ranch required of a woman.

When the tub was full, and the temperature was to her satisfaction, she turned to him. "I'll bath quickly. You won't have to wait outside for more than a half hour."

"I'm not waiting outside." He took a chair at the table and pulled a piece of paper to him. "I won't watch, but I'm not going outside." It was his house, and she was his wife. Why on earth would he go outside?

"But...I can't disrobe in front of you." Gwen couldn't believe he was being so difficult. What would her life be like?

"Why can't you? I'm going to be seeing

you naked for the rest of our lives," he asked reasonably. The woman was crazed.

"You will *not* be seeing me naked! How dare you?" What kind of woman did he think she was?

Walt looked at her again. "How old are you?" She couldn't be more than fifteen if she thought he wouldn't see her naked when they made love.

"I'm twenty-one." How her age was relevant, she didn't know.

"So you know I'll be touching you everywhere tonight, right? Why are you worried about me seeing what I'll be touching in just an hour?"

She gaped at him. "What do you mean you'll be touching me everywhere? I haven't given you permission to even kiss me yet!" He was crazed.

He sighed. "You do know what happens

between a man and a woman when they marry, right?"

"They love each other for all eternity, and he then can kiss her whenever he would like," Gwen answered primly.

Walt groaned. "On second thought, I will go for that walk." He got up and left the house, needing to have one of her sisters talk to her. Thinking about which one would be most appropriate, he stormed to Bart's house. Scrawny Bonnie would be the one to help him. She seemed to know everything.

He pounded on his brother's door, and for the first time ever waited for him to answer before storming inside. He hoped he wasn't interrupting his brother's wedding night, but from the look on Bart's face when he'd met Bonnie, he really didn't need to worry about that.

Bonnie answered the door, peeking out.

"What can I do for you, Mr. Dalton?"

"I'm Walt. Can I talk to you for a minute, Bonnie?" There were delicious smells wafting out of the house. He knew that Bart's larder had been practically bare, and he immediately saw this woman as a sorceress in the kitchen. He could feel the saliva pooling in his mouth and wished he had the right to walk in and eat whatever he wanted.

"Yes, of course." She glanced over her shoulder, and he noticed Bart for the first time, asleep with his head pillowed on his arms at the kitchen table. She took a shawl from a nail by the door and stepped outside. "How can I help you, Mr. Dalton?"

Walt sighed. "It's kind of a delicate subject." How did one ask his new sister-in-law if her sister had any idea of what happened in the marriage bed?

"Just say it. I'm tired, and would like to

go to sleep." She looked as annoyed as she had at the train station, so he desperately hoped she would help him.

"Does Gertie have any idea what happens in the marriage bed?" he asked quickly. He wasn't a shy man, but talking about this subject with his sister-in-law just felt awkward.

Bonnie tilted her head to the side for one moment, studying him. "Who is Gertie?"

"Isn't that my new wife's name?" He should know her name. He sent up a quick prayer that he hadn't gotten it wrong.

"No, it's not. Her name is Gwen." She shook her head at him. "Maybe you were the right man to marry my sister after all. To answer your question, I don't believe she does know about the marriage bed. Why? Is she refusing you?"

Walt shrugged. "I just got the impression

she didn't know. Would you be willing to go to the house and explain things to her? Please?"

Bonnie sighed heavily. "If I must. I suppose it's the least I can do for her since I'm the one who dragged her out here under false pretenses." She motioned for him to go ahead of her. "After you, Mr. Dalton. I'm afraid I don't know which of these pitiful shacks is yours."

Walt glared at her before turning and leading the way to his house. She may be the best cook of the three, but her tongue was so sharp, he wasn't sure he would be able to survive a meal with her.

"She's bathing. I'll wait out here." He opened the door for Bonnie, not looking at his wife. Just the thought of her being in his home, undressed, had him aroused. He didn't need it to be any more obvious around her sister.

Gwen looked up as Bonnie approached. She was half asleep and enjoying her bath immensely. "Bonnie!" Why she'd been certain she'd never see her sisters again, she didn't know, but she had been even after Walt's assurances. "It's so good to see you!" In that moment she forgot all about her anger for Bonnie dragging her to Texas.

Bonnie smiled and pulled up a chair beside Gwen's tub. "Let me wash your hair for you." While she worked at her sister's hair, she asked, "Gwenny? Do you know what happens in the marriage bed?"

Gwen laughed. "What kind of question is that? Of course I do!"

Bonnie eyed her sister skeptically. "You do? Why don't you tell me then? I want to be ready."

"Well, in the marriage bed, the couple

sleeps together every night. It's a way to help bind a couple together." Gwen knew that, because someone had mentioned the marriage bed to her, so she'd asked her mother.

Bonnie sighed. "That's not exactly the whole truth. Did Mama tell you that?"

"Yes, of course."

"Well, there's a bit more to it than that." As soon as she'd finished rinsing her sister's hair, she started washing her back for her. "Here's the whole truth, Gwen..."

By the time Bonnie was finished with her explanation, Gwen's face was burning hot. "Do you think Walton wants me to do that with him? Tonight?" She would die of embarrassment, but he'd said something about seeing her naked. He'd wait for a few years for her to be ready, though, wouldn't he?

"I'm certain he does, Gwen. All men want that on their wedding night." Bonnie got to her feet. "He asked me to come over and explain what would happen to you."

Gwen was still shocked. "Have you done it? With Bart?"

Bonnie shook her head. "No, all we've done is cook a meal, and he kissed me at the wedding."

"Oh. Well, do you know if it hurts?" Gwen tried not to panic about the idea of what was to come, but she needed to know as much as she could so she could prepare herself.

Bonnie shrugged. "I've never done it, but I've been told the first time does hurt some."

"I want to come home with you then. I don't think I feel like doing *that* this evening."

Bonnie shook her head. "You're a married woman now, Gwenny. It's your duty. The Bible says so."

Gwen hated the idea of being in such a vulnerable position with her husband. Why hadn't someone told her about this before she married? "Do you think Libby would let me stay with her?"

"It's not a matter of whether we want you around. It's time for you to fulfill your duty." She took the drying cloth from the table and held it up for her sister. "I'll help you brush your hair dry."

Gwen stepped out of the tub and allowed Bonnie to engulf her in the towel. "I'm scared, Bonnie."

"I know you are. You'll get through it."

Bonnie painstakingly brushed out Gwen's hair.

Walt paced back and forth in front of his cabin, glaring at it. How long did it take to explain? Were they trying to put him off?

He sighed. He was impatient because it had been a long time for him, but he had to keep in mind that he'd married an innocent.

He had to be kind and understanding. Dagnabit. He had to be someone he wasn't. How was he going to do that?

When Bonnie finally left the house, he rushed forward. "Did you explain everything?"

Bonnie nodded, not meeting his gaze. "I'd appreciate it if you walked me home."

Walt nodded. "Absolutely, ma'am." He walked across the lawn to Bart's cabin. "Thank you for taking the time to help me."

"I look at it as helping my sister." When they reached her new front door, she turned to him. "Be patient with her. She's not used to ever hearing the word 'no.'" With that she slipped into the house and closed the door behind her.

He could hear Bart's snores from the yard. What was his brother doing falling asleep at the table on his wedding night?

Walt turned to go back to his own cabin. He said a quick prayer for patience and opened the door. His bride was nowhere to be seen. Was she waiting in bed for him?

He walked into the bedroom, and sure enough, she was curled on her side, fast asleep. He wondered for a moment if he should wake her but decided to let her sleep. He'd wake her early in the morning to start their marriage. He was a strong man and another few hours wouldn't hurt him a lick.

Chapter Four

After breakfast, Gwen stood doing the breakfast dishes. She'd protested to Walton that she'd just done dishes the night before, but he just shook his head at her. "You'll be doing dishes three times a day every day. I'll be home at noon for lunch." He'd kissed her softly and plopped his hat on his head, heading out to work for the day.

She blushed as she thought of how Walt had woken her that morning. The man must have fifteen hands. He was so good at kissing, though. And she'd enjoyed it more than she'd thought possible. Surely he'd hire a maid as soon as they could afford it and rescue her from her life of servitude.

Gwen hated doing the dishes. Maybe if

she learned to cook, Walt would do the dishes. It was at least worth trying, wasn't it?

There was a knock on her door, and Gwen hurried over to open it. Both of her sisters stood in front of her. "Come in!" She wondered how she could get Bonnie to do her dishes for her without coming right out and asking.

Bonnie looked over at the basin and smiled. "I see you're almost finished with the dishes. I came over to bake bread for the next two days. You two need to learn to cook as soon as you can so you can please your husbands."

Gwen knew she'd pleased her husband without knowing how to cook, but she said nothing. What could she say? *I can please my husband in bed just as well as I please him in the kitchen?* She could just imagine her sister's reaction to that statement.

She rushed over and finished the dishes, looking forward to learning to cook. Anything to get out of dish duty.

The three sisters talked about their husbands the whole while. "Nate was angry with me for refusing to share the marriage bed with him. I made him sleep on the floor. I told him he'd have to woo me."

Gwen blushed. How had Libby managed to keep Nate from doing *that* with her? She'd certainly tried with Walt, but he'd been very insistent. Of course, now that she'd done it, she wouldn't complain about doing it again.

Gwen held her tongue. She wasn't going to say a word. Her sisters didn't need to know that she'd enjoyed what she and Walt had done together.

She put the last dish into the cabinet and hurried to the table, sitting with her sisters. "I want to know everything there is to know about cooking," Gwen announced, deliberately changing the subject. "Do you think you could teach us everything today?" She had visions of putting a beautiful meal on the table in front of Walt that evening, and him kissing her feet, promising her he'd wash every single dish in their home for the rest of their marriage.

Bonnie laughed. "I took lessons from Mrs. Butterfield for a year. I can't teach all that in one day."

Gwen sighed. "You'll teach us as fast as you can, though, right?"

Bonnie nodded. "I'll walk you through cooking meals this week, and I'll write everything down from now on. You'll learn fast. The cooking we'll do here will be much simpler than it was back in Beckham." She waved to the stove. "At least we won't have to use fireplaces. I do know how to cook on one, though."

They spent the morning mixing the dough for bread. Gwen was shocked by the muscles required to knead the dough. She hadn't ever thought of cooking as something that required a lot of physical strength.

By the time the loaves were in the pans and rising, Gwen was covered in flour from head to toe. She sat in the chair and sighed. "That was a lot of work. I'm hungry." Looking at Bonnie, she asked, "What's for lunch?"

Bonnie laughed. "We all need to make lunch for our husbands. Whatever you make is what you'll have." She walked toward the door. "I'll be back this afternoon to help you bake the loaves and to help with supper."

Libby was right behind her and she closed the door after them.

Gwen looked at the door and sighed. She

wondered if Walt would be satisfied with a sandwich for lunch. Surely there was something she could make into a sandwich. She went into the cellar to see if she could find something down there.

Finding a slab of bacon, she carried it up the narrow steps and set it on the worktable. She found a knife and carefully cut off strips. She had no idea what she was doing, but she was determined to make lunch for her husband.

She put a pan in the middle of the stove that she'd had going all morning. She put the thick slices of bacon on the stove and cut up the last of the bread he had sitting on the work table. Hopefully it was still good, because the bread she was making with her sisters wouldn't be ready until later that afternoon.

She stood over the bacon with a fork, turning it every minute in the hopes it would cook faster and not burn. She'd never cooked anything in her life, so she had no idea if she was going about it the right way.

The door opened and closed behind her. "Lunch isn't ready yet?"

Gwen held her breath for a moment instead of turning and unleashing her fury on Walt. She couldn't believe he was criticizing her when he had no idea what she had done all morning. Why, she'd never done that much work in a month, much less in a morning.

She turned to him with a smile, getting her temper under control at last. "It's almost ready. We're having bacon sandwiches."

"I see that." He nodded to the plates with bread sliced on them. "Do you want me to butter the bread?"

She nodded. "Yes, please. It'll taste better that way."

Walt looked at the loaves of bread lined up on the work table and saw a lot of sandwiches in his future. At least he'd be fed and not have to do any of the dishes for a change. She could be a good wife with a little training, and her sister seemed to be just the right woman to do that training.

He got up and got the butter and the bread she'd sliced, buttering each piece of bread. There wasn't much of the store bought butter left, so he certainly hoped she knew how to make it. He didn't have a butter churn, and neither did his brothers, but they lived close enough that they could spend the money on just one and share it between the three couples.

Walt smiled at the back of his wife's head. Gertie may not be much of a cook, but she was easy on the eyes, and just what he was looking for in the bedroom. He was glad her sister had been willing to explain everything, because he wasn't certain he could have explained it all in a way that would have satisfied the pretty little thing.

She put a plate of bacon on the table, and he eyed it skeptically as he buttered the last piece of bread. There were undercooked parts and overcooked parts...all on the same slice. How did she do that? It took skill to cook something that poorly.

She stood over it as proudly as if she'd just shot, skinned, and cooked a bear all on her own, so he didn't complain. "Looks good," he lied.

Gwen smiled happily. "I've never cooked anything before. I hope it tastes as good as it looks."

She slipped into the chair across from him, and he took her hand in his as he prayed over their meal. He added a silent prayer that neither of them would die from her cooking. "I'm hungry enough to eat my horse," he told her.

"What did you do this morning?" she asked.

He shrugged. "Built fences. We've got one section of land all fenced off, but we need to be able to move the herd. There are no other sections that have been prepared, so we're working on that now. We want there to be five or six different pastures to move the cattle between."

Gwen had no idea why they would want to do that, but at that moment she didn't care. She took her first bite of her bacon sandwich and all but cringed. It was terrible. She started to push it away, but when she saw that he was eating every bite as if it was actually good, she decided she could force herself to do the same.

He talked about the ranch while they ate, and she nodded a lot as if she was actually listening. She wanted to go into town and explore. "What's the nearest town?" she asked.

He grinned. "Wiggieville. Isn't that a crazy name?"

"It is. How far is it?" She wasn't about to ask how that town got its name, but she was sure someone would volunteer the information soon.

"About an hour drive from here. If you ladies want to go, let me know, and I'll have Bart take you in." He'd send Bart because he thought Bart was the one who needed the most time with his lady. His brother had looked very unhappy that morning, and he was certain it was the lack of marital relations.

Gwen pushed back from the table and

walked to the basin. She set the water she'd brought in earlier on to boil. She'd do the dishes, even though she'd cooked. The meal had been almost inedible, and it wouldn't be fair to ask Walt to do the dishes for her. After supper she'd make him wash them. That would be fair. Because she was going to make him the best meal he'd ever eaten.

*****

While they worked on the fences that afternoon, Walt asked the brothers what they thought of their new wives. He'd not been willing to broach the subject that morning, because he knew they were still a bit angry with him for not telling them they were getting married.

"Lizzy's a pretty little thing," he said to Nate.

Nate nodded. "Libby sure is. Wish she could cook, though."

Walt sighed. Would they only find fault with their wives? At least he'd provided them helpers. Their dynasty couldn't be built without wives. "What do you think of Bonnie, Bart? She can cook!"

Bart shrugged. "She sure can. She's a fine woman, and any man would be lucky to have her as a wife. You two lost out when you didn't pick her."

Walt grunted. "Well, Gertie may not be able to cook, but she's gorgeous, and she's willing to learn to work hard." He couldn't call her a hard worker at that point, because she obviously wasn't. He needed to make it clear that their wives were good women, though.

Nate laughed. "The only one of them that knows how to work is Bonnie, and all three of us know it." He looked at Walt. "And why do you keep calling your wife Gertie? Her name is Gwen."

Walt frowned. "Are you sure? I was certain her name was Gertie." He wasn't great with names, but he knew his own wife's name, didn't he?

Bart shook his head at his eldest brother. "You don't even know your wife's name. That's a right shame there, Walt."

Walt said nothing. He'd figure out if they were right later. Hopefully before he accidentally called her by the wrong name. Why couldn't he remember who she was?

Chapter Five

They quickly fell into a routine with the men leaving early to work every morning, and the three women gathering in one of the houses for Bonnie to give the other two some much needed cooking lessons. The only day that was different was Sunday.

Gwen walked into church on their first Sunday there a bit nervous. She'd never attended church as a married woman, and she wasn't certain about the reception she would receive. She was used to men crowding around her as soon as she walked into the building, but would that be the same now that she was married?

As Walton introduced her to the people in the small congregation, she felt more and more relaxed. Why, it was a group of almost entirely single men. She'd have no problem here at all. She knew how to deal with bachelors.

One particular man made her uncomfortable with his knowing looks. "So nice to meet you, ma'am. I'm John Jenkins."

Gwen smiled and held her hand out for him to shake. "I'm Gwen Blue. I mean, Gwen Dalton." She blushed at her mistake. It was the first time she'd ever introduced herself with her married name, though, so she was certain everyone would forgive her.

John took her hand and brought it to his lips. "It will be so nice to have a beautiful lady to look at on Sunday mornings."

Gwen snatched her hand away. She was a married woman now! Why would he do that? She looked around until she found Walt. He didn't seem to be watching which thrilled her.

She didn't know how he'd react to someone like that.

Libby and Bonnie flanked her as John smiled.

Gwen shook her head. "I'm a married woman, Mr. Jenkins."

He shrugged. "Men die young out here. Just staking my claim." He tipped his hat at the three ladies and wandered off.

Libby glared at Gwen. "You can't encourage the men here, Gwenny. None of us need the kind of scandal we had at home!"

Gwen felt sadness overwhelming her. Everyone immediately assumed she was at fault for everything. "I didn't encourage him, Libby. He walked up to me and introduced himself, and the next thing I knew he was kissing my hand. I certainly didn't *ask* him to!"

Libby looked skeptical even as Bonnie

patted her arm. "I'm sorry. It was unfair of us to assume you'd done something wrong without knowing all the facts."

Gwen gave her sister a brief nod and wandered across the church to where Walt stood talking to the preacher, who immediately turned his attention to her. "It's good to see you again, Mrs. Dalton."

Walt smiled proudly, his arm going around her shoulders. "She certainly is nice to look at, isn't she?"

The pastor laughed while Gwen blushed. She didn't think men should be talking about her appearance now that she was a married woman.

"It's time to take your seats," the pastor told them before he wandered to the front of the church.

Gwen followed Walt to a pew in the middle off to the right of the church. Her sisters and brothers-in-law moved into the same pew. Bonnie looked so happy as she stood holding Bart's arm for the song. Gwen was glad her sister had found someone to love her. She deserved it.

After church, Libby asked the others to come over. "Bonnie is making lunch, but I have the best table for company. We thought it would be nice to have all six of us sit down for lunch together."

It was really the first time all six had been together since the wedding. Gwen nodded happily, pleased to be able to eat someone else's cooking. Her own made her stomach hurt.

"I just made a stew, and there are fresh biscuits. I thought we'd all like to be together," Bonnie added.

Walt shrugged. He knew the women got together every day while he and his brothers worked, so he didn't understand why they wanted to be together on their day of rest, but he wasn't going to argue. "Sounds fine."

"Do you need me to bring anything, Bonnie?" Gwen asked, praying her sister would say 'no.' She had no idea what she'd cook for them, because she only cooked what Bonnie told her to cook. She knew it was the right thing to do to offer, though.

Bonnie seemed to think about it for a moment. "You have some jam in your cellar. Why don't you bring that for the biscuits?"

Gwen smiled and sighed with relief. "I'll do that."

On the drive home Gwen asked about taking a trip into town. "We really need a butter churn. Bonnie promised us she'd teach us to make butter if we can just talk you men into a churn. I need to get some fabric as well. Bonnie's promised me a new dress." A cornflower blue dress to be exact, but she wasn't going to tell Walt that. She wanted to look her best for him, and she couldn't wait to see his face when she wore a dress that matched her eyes so perfectly.

Walt nodded. "You don't make your own dresses?" Did she do any kind of work?

Gwen looked down at her hands. Somehow Walt made her feel as if she'd wasted her life before meeting him. She hated that. "I've never learned. Bonnie's promised to teach me, though."

Walt sighed. "What exactly did you do all day before you came out here?"

Gwen frowned. She'd been locked in her room for two full months before moving to Texas, but she didn't want to tell him about that or the scandal that had preceded it. "I spent time shopping, talking to my sisters, visiting with friends. That's what young ladies do back East."

"Then why does Bonnie know how to do everything while you know how to do nothing? You had the same mother, I presume." He couldn't tell by looks or actions, though. The two women were as different as night and day.

Gwen sighed. "We did have the same mother, and she encouraged each of us in our strengths. Bonnie is smart, and she was always good at cooking and sewing. So Mama had someone teach her to be even better at those things. I was always the pretty one, so she taught me to shop for clothes that suited me best, and I learned how to style my hair in the most attractive ways." As she said the words, she thought of a way she could help Bonnie if Bonnie would accept her help. She could teach her sister how to style her hair in a more flattering way.

"So your mother didn't work with you at all on cooking or sewing?" He was surprised to hear that. He'd never heard of a young lady who wasn't taught to do those things at least some.

"Well...she tried. I just wasn't a very good pupil." She wasn't a willing pupil either. Now she really wished she'd listened to her mother when she'd told her she'd need to be able to cook someday. When she watched Bonnie it was as if her sister was able to do it all without thinking. She needed to be that way someday.

Walt shook his head, sure he understood completely. His wife had been spoiled beyond anything he'd ever seen, and she didn't care to work hard to do better. He could see her complaining about it too. "I see."

Gwen really hoped he didn't see. He was the most handsome man she'd ever spent time with, and he was her husband. She wanted him to think only the best of her, of course. She took his arm and rested her cheek on his shoulder as he drove. Maybe she could distract him from thinking about it too much.

When they pulled into the yard in front of Libby's house, Walt helped Gwen down and then went to take care of the horses. "You go on in. It's too cold for you to stay outside for long."

Gwen wanted to laugh at that. It was a balmy day. They only had days like this in Massachusetts in the summer. Never in the middle of October. "All right." She did her best to sound obedient.

First she rushed home to get two jars of jam. She wasn't certain where Walt had gotten them, but they were good. She carried them to Libby's house and went inside.

Libby's cabin was the only one that really

felt finished to her. It had beautiful furnishings, like Nate had a woman in mind when he chose them. She knew that wasn't the case with Walt. Walt had chosen the things that were most suitable for his lifestyle, whether they would be pleasing to a woman's eye or not. He was a frugal man, determined to spend his money where it mattered most and would do him the most good, which meant he put his money into his herd.

Bonnie's was the worst, though. She felt bad for Bonnie. Bart had barely enough for him to survive, and when you added in a wife? That must be hard. The couple seemed happy together though. Bonnie was always smiling, and when they were together, they were always holding hands or she was holding his arm. Walt wasn't that demonstrative in public, and Gwen found herself envious of her sister for the first time in her life.

Gwen placed the jam on the table and walked over to Bonnie who was standing guard over a huge pot at the stove, while Libby sat at the table watching. "Do you need any help?"

Bonnie shook her head. "Not really. You two can set the table if you'd like, but there's really nothing else to do."

Libby smiled and rushed over to a chest of drawers where she kept her dishes and silverware. She pulled out a tablecloth and napkins. It wasn't long before Libby and Gwen had the table looking every bit as pretty as their table at home had looked.

When they were finished, Libby took a step back and eyed the table. "It needs something, doesn't it?"

Gwen shrugged, knowing she didn't have the ability to make her table look half as good no matter how hard she tried. She just didn't have the pretty dishes and silverware.

A moment later the men came into the house, all of them wiping their feet and hanging their hats on hooks by the door. "For my beautiful wife," Nate said, pulling a small bouquet of wildflowers from behind his back.

Libby clapped her hands together once. "That's just what we needed!" She ran and got a vase, filled it with water, and tucked the flowers into it. Putting the arrangement onto the center of the table, she smiled and nodded. "Isn't that better, Gwen?"

Gwen nodded, suddenly feeling inadequate. She'd always been a bit jealous of Libby but never like she was at that moment. Libby was the best of both of her sisters. She was pretty and smart. Gwen had the looks, but she didn't have the brains to go with them. She sighed. She did have the brains. She'd just never done anything to develop them.

"Table's set, Bonnie. Anything else we can do?" Gwen asked, trying not to think about anything.

"Coffee's ready. Why don't you pour a cup for everyone, Gwen?" Bonnie suggested.

When they were all seated at the table, Walt said, "I'll pray for us." His prayer was simple and to the point. "Thank you for bringing us women who will share our lives with us. Thank you for this food. Amen."

The others echoed the 'amen' and then passed the dishes. Gwen had never eaten with her brothers-in-law before and she studied them all, looking for ways to tell them apart.

Bart was the easiest. He was leaner than the other two, as if he hadn't always had quite enough food. His hair was also a bit longer.

Nate and Walton were just alike though, so she started looking for distinguishing marks. It wouldn't do for her not to be able to tell them apart on sight. Walt's shoulders were a little broader, and his tan was a tad bit darker. They would have to be standing beside each other for her to tell that difference in them, though.

Finally she realized how she'd be able to tell them apart. Walt had a tiny cowlick just above his right ear. Four or five strands of hair stood out straight from his head. She sighed. If that was the only way to tell them apart, then she'd make it work.

They talked as they ate, the men telling their stories. They'd been raised by a dairy farmer and his wife. Their father had once gone to the gold mines to make his fortune, but he'd come home with only enough money to buy the family farm and enough cows to make a living.

They'd been raised not really in poverty,

but they had always known the burden of hard work, even as young boys.

Bonnie told them about their merchant father and how they had three brothers Brett, Hank and Percy.

Gwen thought about her brothers as Bonnie mentioned them. She missed them, which surprised her. Bret was the oldest, and he was the one who tended to be the bossiest. He thought his younger siblings were put on earth to do his bidding. The sisters all called him Bossy Brett. The middle brother was Hank, who had helped them escape. He was incredibly handsome. He and Gwen turned every head when they walked down the street together. Percy was the youngest and most annoying of the three in Gwen's mind. He did everything he was told immediately. He was perfect in every way.

"I left home at seventeen," Bart told them.

"I don't know why, but I just couldn't stay there any longer. My feet have always been itchy."

Gwen frowned. "Why do your feet itch?"

Bart sighed. "It's an expression. I have a hard time staying in one place for a long time. I prefer to move around and see new things. I hate seeing the same thing day in and day out."

"You're a rambler," Gwen said, her eyes widening. She looked at Bonnie, but his words didn't seem to surprise her sister.

Bart shrugged. "I prefer the term 'drifter.'"

"Drifter. All right." She looked at Nate. "What about you?"

"I've traveled a lot as well, but I don't have a problem staying in one place as long as things are going well. I've been a cowboy my entire life. I really never dreamed I'd have my own spread, but when Walt suggested this, we had to join him." Nate shrugged. "There's a bond between us. When one of us needs something, the others are always there."

Bonnie eyed Nate for a moment before nodding. "What about you, Walt? What have you been doing since you left your parents' home?"

Walt smiled. "Learning everything I can about life and about ranching. I knew someday I'd end up somewhere with my brothers, and we'd build our own empire. It's happening now."

"Empire?" Gwen asked. He dreamed big.

"Empire. How does it feel to be an empress, darlin'?"

Chapter Six

After breakfast the following morning, Bart drove the three sisters into town. He'd kindly added a plank onto the back so there would be a second seat, and she and Libby wouldn't have to sit in the wagon bed.

Gwen thanked him for handing her up into the wagon. "Thanks for driving us to town."

Bart nodded, but said nothing.

"Why are you driving us?" Libby asked. "Wouldn't it have made more sense for you to stay and work while we went to town?"

Bart shrugged. "It would, but we decided I needed to go with you the first few times you head to town. You're not back East any longer, ladies. Out here men outnumber women. It's not safe for a lady to be wandering around town alone."

"We'd have each other," Gwen argued. She truly didn't have a problem with Bart driving them just this once. They didn't know the way to Wiggieville, so it made sense that they didn't drive themselves. Doing it every time *didn't* make sense, though. Gwen was used to her independence. After being locked in her room for two months, she was now in Texas under the watchful eye of her brother-in-law. Was this any way to treat an empress?

"Maybe eventually you'll get to go alone. For now, I'm driving you." His tone of voice made it clear that he wouldn't respond to any other arguments.

Bonnie was sitting close to him, clutching his arm. "I appreciate you looking out for us, Bart."

Gwen rolled her eyes at Libby who

giggled. They watched the scenery as they drove. Gwen was thrilled to have a day off from cooking lessons. As much as she wanted to learn to cook well, the actual learning made her crazy. Bonnie was a hard taskmaster.

When they got to town, Bart helped them all down. "I'll wait in the wagon," he told them.

Gwen was happy to hear that. She didn't want to have her brother-in-law breathing down her neck while she browsed the only store they had available to them.

Once inside, Gwen was severely disappointed. There weren't half as many items for sale here as there were back home. While Bonnie and Libby picked out a butter churn, Gwen looked through the fabrics. There weren't many choices. Finally, at the bottom of the table, she found a bolt of cornflower blue material with tiny little flowers on it. She tucked it under her arm with a huge smile, carrying it over to her sisters.

Bonnie and Libby already had a whole pile of supplies on the counter ready to purchase. "We'll need flour, sugar, and lard as well." She turned to her sisters. "Should we get some potatoes? We need to plan what we're going to make for Thanksgiving."

Gwen nodded. "That's still a whole month away, but we can start talking about it. Are we going to eat at Libby's?"

"She has the best place for entertaining." Bonnie sighed. "I can't wait until spring when we can put our kitchen gardens in. We'll have so much more to choose from."

When they were ready, Bonnie went out to get Bart to tote things out to the wagon. After she left, Gwen turned to the merchant.

"Is there a post office nearby? I need to mail a letter to my Aunt Edna." Her aunt lived in Seattle, and though they'd never met, they'd been carrying on a correspondence for years.

"I take care of the mail in town," he told her.

Gwen handed her letter to him before turning to speak with Libby. "It's nice to be able to shop, even if it's only for a little while in a tiny store."

Libby nodded. "It is! We'll have to work harder than ever this afternoon to make up for it, though. Bonnie said she was going to teach us to wash clothes tomorrow."

Gwen shuddered. "I don't even want to think about washing the yellow dress I came here in. It's rank."

"I don't think there's any way we'll be able to convince Bonnie to do it for us." Libby frowned, obviously thinking of her own travel clothes.

"I know. I wish we were rich, and we could just hire someone to do everything." Gwen frowned. She knew she should be happy to be in Texas, married to a handsome rancher, instead of back home married to old man Bellafonte. "Not that I'm not happy with Walton."

Libby nodded. "I understand exactly what you mean. Walt seems like a good man."

Gwen nodded. "Oh, he is. He's just...larger than life sometimes. I really think he thinks everyone should be able to do everything he can, plus a million other things. I'd like to see something he's not good at just once, you know? He even cooks better than I do."

"Gwen honey? The horses cook better than you do. You need to start applying yourself when Bonnie teaches us."

"There's no need to be rude, Libby."

"Sometimes there is," Libby argued. "Sometimes you need to hear that you can't be a spoiled brat here. We're all going to need to work hard if we're going to make the empire Walt has in his head a reality. You say all the right things, but you don't really try while Bonnie is teaching us. You're so convinced you can't do it that you just don't."

Gwen frowned. "That's not true. I try really hard." Was her sister right? Had she decided she couldn't cook well so she wasn't even trying?

"Sometimes, you're your own worst enemy. Being pretty doesn't get the food cooked or the laundry done. Bonnie's willing to teach us, but she's not going to spend all her time teaching us forever, you know." Libby turned as Bonnie came back into the store with Bart right behind her.

Gwen picked up her fabric and carried it out to the wagon while she thought about her sister's words. She couldn't live on her looks any longer. Libby was right. It was time for her to get her hands dirty whether she liked it or not.

*****

Gwen made a roast for dinner that evening while Bonnie watched over her. She carefully peeled all the potatoes to tuck into the pot with the meat, and even peeled the carrots by herself. As soon as the roast was in the oven, Bonnie said it was time to bake bread again. For the first time, Gwen didn't complain. She was going to be the best wife she could be, if only to prove she wasn't spoiled.

She couldn't believe her own sisters didn't

think she was trying to be a good wife. Didn't they know her better than that?

When she served the dinner she'd fixed herself that evening, she smiled as she saw Walton sniff his plate and smile. "This smells wonderful!"

"I did it all myself. Bonnie told me what to do, but I did it." She couldn't keep the pride out of her voice as she told him it was all her doing.

"Well, you obviously did a good job. It smells great." He was pleased to hear she was ready to stop letting her sister do everything. He wanted a wife who could do her chores without instruction.

Gwen slipped into her chair across from Walt and waited while he prayed for them both. She took a bite of the meat and smiled. "It actually tastes good!"

He laughed and took a bite himself. "Yes,

it does. Very good!" He served himself a helping of the boiled potatoes and added gravy to them. The gravy had a few lumps which told him she must have made it after Bonnie had left.

Overall the meal was the best she'd made. The carrots were a bit hard, but he didn't care. She was improving. "This meal is wonderful. Thank you for your hard work."

Gwen felt like dancing around the house at his praise. He wasn't one to praise falsely, so she felt really good about herself. While they ate, she thought back to his words of the day before. "Did you mean what you said yesterday? About building an empire?"

He nodded. "Absolutely. We have enough land to grow a huge herd. We're less than a year into this, and we've already made a bit of money. I've got quite a bit saved from my years of working for other men. We've got a good start on it."

"Do you think we'll have a big house some day?"

Walt laughed. "We'll have a house fit for an empress, of course. What I see is having one huge house with three spokes going out the sides and back. Each of us could raise our family in one of the spokes."

"Spokes?" Gwen wasn't following his line of thought.

He got up from the table and got a piece of paper, sitting back down to draw it out for her. He drew a huge square, and coming off of the back and each of the two sides were long halls with rooms off of them. "Like this. We'd live in this spoke," he said, pointing to the hall off the right side of the building. "Bonnie and Bart would live off the back, and Nate and Libby would live off this side. We'd share all the common areas. In each spoke we'll have a large bedroom, a nursery, maybe two small bedrooms and a bathroom. We'll all share the parlors and the kitchen."

She chuckled. "It sounds nice. Have your brothers agreed to this plan yet?"

He shook his head. "No, of course not. I haven't even mentioned it to them. They'll do it if I ask though. I'm the oldest."

She raised an eyebrow. "You're triplets. How can being the oldest matter when you're triplets?"

He shrugged. "I can't answer that really, but it always has. When we were children, they did whatever I said. When I moved here and decided to ranch, I sent them both a letter asking them to come. Asking was just a formality, though. I knew they'd come if I asked them to."

"So you're the leader of the three of you?" She didn't quite understand. She would never do everything Bonnie asked, just because her sister asked it. Bonnie was bossy, like every oldest child she'd ever known, but that didn't mean she was going to follow her blindly.

"Not exactly. I'm not sure how to explain it. Being triplets, we're connected in a way most siblings aren't. I think we all knew that one day we'd end up living close together and working together. It's just the way things were meant to be."

Gwen didn't understand but decided not to question him further. It was odd to her way of thinking, but if it made them happy, then who was she to judge?

After dinner, they sat and talked for a few minutes, and she waited for him to volunteer to do the dishes, because she'd worked so hard cooking. When he didn't, she got to her feet and did them herself. It was obviously going to continue to be her job until they could hire a maid or she had daughters she could pass the chore on to.

When she was finished, she turned to see him watching her. He had that little sparkle in his eye that told her what he wanted, and he always wanted the same thing. "Are we going to make an early night of it again?" she asked as he got to his feet and stalked toward her.

He picked her up and carried her into the bedroom, setting her gently on the bed. "Always, my dear."

Chapter Seven

Gwen fell deeper and deeper in love with Walton every day of their marriage. There was just something compelling about him, something that made her want to be more than she was. Every day she got up a little earlier and worked a little harder.

The first time she baked bread without Bonnie giving her instructions, she danced around the room, kissing her older sister on the cheek. "You're a wonderful teacher, Bonnie!"

Bonnie smiled. "You've been trying hard. That makes a big difference."

Gwen looked over at Libby who was nodding and smiling. "I'm really glad you decided to work so hard, Gwen. Walt must be so proud of you."

Gwen blushed. "I think he is." Whether he was proud or not, she knew he was very happy with her body. Every night he carried her off to bed and made love to her. Most mornings, she woke with him stroking her insistently. "I'm happy."

The words stunned her as she said them. She'd never thought she could be happy doing as much manual labor as she did. Or without having a man dote on her every whim. Walt was not one to treat her with kid gloves. He expected her to work just as hard as he did, which was harder than she'd ever imagined anyone worked. Somehow, though, being in Texas and working so hard was making her happy. Of course, she was certain much of it was Walt. He made her happy just by being him.

Bonnie looked at Gwen and smiled.

"Well of course you are. We all are. We married good men. I'm sure Libby is happy too."

Libby nodded, a smile plastered to her face. It didn't look absolutely true to Gwen, but she wasn't going to contradict her sisters.

"For me, I think it's more than that," Gwen told the others. "I think I finally feel like I'm doing something worthwhile."

Bonnie laughed. "You mean you're not spending all day every day gadding about with your friends and every evening with a different beau? Yes, you're doing something much more worthwhile than that."

Gwen frowned. She had been somewhat worthless before. She could see it now, but she hadn't been able to then. When they'd been at home, she'd felt like the entire world revolved around her. As if other people were only put on the planet to make her happy.

Now, she did everything she could to make others happy, and not just her husband. She worked hard to make her sisters and their husbands happy as well.

"What are we cooking for dinner tonight?" Gwen asked, wanting to change the subject from the selfish girl she'd been.

Bonnie shrugged. "Bart's away for a few days, so I'll probably just have a sandwich."

Gwen frowned. "Where did he go?" Bonnie and Bart seemed so happy together. She must miss him terribly.

Bonnie smiled. "Oh, he had to go on a business trip."

"I didn't hear about that." Gwen looked at Libby. "Did Nate go as well?"

Libby shook her head. "Nate told me that Bart is always the one to go on business trips. He and Walt never go."

"Never? Really?" Gwen frowned. "That

doesn't seem fair." She didn't want Walt to have to be the one to leave, but it would be more fair than Bart leaving every time one of them had to go somewhere.

Libby shrugged. "He said all three of them prefer it that way."

"How odd." Gwen sat down and thought for a moment. "Maybe I'll make a big pot of soup. Isn't there a potato soup that you know how to make, Bonnie?"

"Oh, yes. I have a wonderful recipe for a potato soup. I'll teach you both to make it this evening."

Gwen paid close attention as Bonnie showed them how to make the soup, giving them each something to do to help her. She watched her sister, and she noticed she seemed sad. She wanted to ask her about it, but she was afraid to. She didn't want to pry. If her sister wanted to talk to her, she would.

She was probably just missing her husband.

Before her sisters left for the evening to go to their own homes, Gwen asked, "Do you want to stay for supper, Bonnie? We'd love to have you." She hated the idea of her sister eating alone.

Bonnie considered for a moment. "Walt won't mind?"

"Of course not. Please come." Gwen really hoped she wasn't speaking out of turn. Walt did enjoy their evenings alone, but surely he'd see that her sister shouldn't have to be alone.

Bonnie nodded. "I'd be happy to. I have something for you anyway. Let me run home and get it."

Libby smiled at Gwen once their sister was gone. "Thank you for inviting her. I was just about to. I don't want her eating by herself."

Gwen hugged Libby impulsively. "We think alike at times, little sister."

Libby left then, and Gwen cut one of the loaves of bread they'd made that day, putting a fresh ball of butter on the table. She was proud of that ball of butter. Her arms still ached from the hours of churning, but it tasted delicious.

Bonnie was back minutes later. Gwen had finished setting the table and was whipping some cream to put on top of the cake they'd made earlier. It was Gwen's first cake, and she was worried that it wouldn't be perfect for Walt.

Bonnie walked in with something wrapped in brown paper in her arms and tied with a string. "For you."

Gwen stared at it in surprise. "It's not my birthday."

Bonnie laughed. "No, it's not. Open it."

Gwen sat at the table and opened the package. It was her cornflower blue dress, and it was just as beautiful as Gwen had dreamed it would be. "Oh, Bonnie! It's perfect. When did you find the time? We're working morning to night."

Bonnie shrugged. "I've been doing it in the evenings after supper. I can always find a little time."

Gwen's time after supper was taken up by dishes and Walt. If he was around, she was doing something with him. "Thank you so much. I'm going to run and put it on right now." She rushed into the bedroom to change.

Walt opened the door from his long day. Bart had gone off again, drifting around the area, and they'd had to work harder to make up for him not being there. He was exhausted.

The first thing he saw when he opened the door was Bonnie standing at the stove, stirring something. He sighed. Wasn't Gwen doing her share now? He'd thought she was working harder. He hung his hat on its peg and hung his coat. "Where's Gwen?"

"Oh, she's changing for supper. She'll be right out."

"You didn't have to cook for us, Bonnie." Walt felt as if he needed to apologize for his wife's laziness. Didn't she know it was her job to cook for them?

"I didn't! Gwen cooked. I just supervised. She invited me to stay for supper because Bart is on his business trip."

Walt raised an eyebrow at the mention of a business trip. Did Bonnie really think that's where he was, or was she just saving face?

Gwen stepped out of the bedroom, wearing a pretty new dress. "Look what

177

Bonnie made for me. She left my favorite dress behind, and she made another almost exactly like it to make up for it."

Walt smiled. "It looks good on you." He walked across the room and kissed her cheek. You look beautiful." He turned to Bonnie. "You'll need to teach her to sew soon as well."

Bonnie smiled. "She's done some small things. She'll work up to dresses." She automatically started to serve their supper, but Gwen shooed her.

"No, you're our guest this evening. You sit down, and I'll serve us all." Gwen put her apron on and set the soup on the table. "It's the first time I've made this, so I hope it's good." Had Walt been complaining about her lack of work? She hoped not. She'd ask him about it later.

Bonnie stayed after supper, helping Gwen wash the dishes. Gwen told her not to, but

Bonnie insisted on helping. "You fixed dinner. It's the least I can do."

When they were finished, Walt stood. "I'll walk you home." He knew it wasn't far, but he couldn't let a lady walk alone in the dark.

Bonnie looked for a moment like she was going to argue, but she nodded. "I'd appreciate that."

When he returned, Gwen was already in her nightgown brushing out her hair. He walked up behind her and pressed his lips to the side of her neck.

"Were you worried that I wasn't doing my share?" she asked quietly, not wanting to forget to have the conversation.

Walt felt bad for doubting her but knew he needed to answer honestly. "Only a little. You've been doing so well, and I was worried you were going back to your old ways."

"What were my old ways?" Gwen carefully kept her voice even. Did he realize how selfish she used to be?

How could he answer that without hurting her feelings? "Well, it's pretty obvious that before you came here you'd never worked a day in your life. Bonnie's obviously a very hard worker, so I assume it was just you and not her."

Gwen nodded. "Yes, but I explained that."

He shrugged. "If you'd wanted to work, no one would have stopped you. People don't stop others from working hard. It just doesn't happen."

Gwen felt like crying. He was right, but she didn't want him to know that about her. "I suppose."

Walt took her face in his hands, looking deep into her eyes. "I care for you, Gwen.

You are one of the most beautiful women I've ever met, and you're a good wife to me. Please don't think I'm criticizing you."

Gwen sighed. "I don't. I just...well, I know I wasn't as good as I should have been. I was too selfish." She leaned forward to softly kiss his lips. "I hope you know that I've changed."

He nodded. "I do know that. I've watched you grow in the time you've been here, and I'm very proud of the woman you're becoming. Now you're not only beautiful, but you're a hard worker and a loving wife."

Was he saying he loved her? Or that he knew she loved him? Either way, he deserved to hear the words from her. "I love you, Walton Dalton. Thank you for bringing me here and making me your wife."

Walt swept her into his arms and carried her to his bed. There he proceeded to make sweet love to her. He must have done something right to deserve this special woman in his life.

*****

While she was working with her sisters the following afternoon, learning to sew this time, there was a noise outside, and all three sisters dropped the curtains they were making for Bonnie's cabin and rushed to the tiny windows. There was a woman in a fancy carriage, who looked to be swollen with child.

Gwen opened the door and stepped outside. Walt had told her to open the door for no one, but it was a pregnant woman. How could she hurt her? "May I help you?" Her sisters flanked her as she faced the older woman.

"I'm here to see Walton Dalton." The

woman, obviously a woman of ill-repute in her low-cut dress that had her breasts toppling out of it, stared down at Gwen with amusement in her eyes. It was as if she found Gwen to be unworthy of her time.

"I'm Gwen Dalton. How may I help you?" Gwen felt each of her sisters take one of her hands, as if they knew what was about to come.

"I'm Lela Mason. I'm here to see Walton about our baby." Lela patted her huge belly with a smug smile.

Gwen took a deep breath. How did one handle a situation such as this? She'd never imagined she would have to deal with a former mistress. "I'll let Walt know you came by. Where are you staying?"

Lela frowned, obviously annoyed she hadn't gotten more of a reaction. "I'm staying here, of course. With the father of my child."

"That's where I put my foot down, Miss Mason. You can stay in town at the hotel, or you can camp on the prairie. I don't care where you go or what you do, but you're not stepping foot under my roof." Gwen folded her arms across her chest and glared at the woman in front of her. She wasn't going to run off crying. She would stand her ground. At least until Walt got home, and then there was no telling what she'd do.

"You're going to refuse to give your husband's child shelter?" Lela looked at her as if she knew Gwen would back down.

"Of course not. As soon as that child is out of your body, I will shelter it with no problem. I'm refusing to give *you* shelter, Miss Mason." Gwen spun on her heel and walked into the house.

When she got inside she clenched her fists and walked into her bedroom, shielded from her sisters by the curtain that hung from the ceiling at least for a moment. Why would Walt send for a wife if he already had a woman who was pregnant with his child? Shouldn't he just have married her? Did he want her to mother his illegitimate child? She wished he was there at that moment so she could throw something at his head.

When she walked back into the main room, she sat down at the table and picked up the curtain she'd been hemming as if nothing was happening. "I'll be staying at your house tonight after I've had a little talk with my husband, Bonnie."

Bonnie nodded. "Don't you think you should give him a chance to explain?"

"Absolutely not. Her swollen belly explained everything as far as I'm concerned. How he could be interested in that...that tart, I don't know. Did he want me as a wife just so he could have a mother for his bastard?"

Libby gasped. "Watch your language, Gwen!"

Gwen glared at Libby. "When your husband's former lover shows up pregnant with his child, you will have every right to chastise me if you behave better than I am now. Until then? You may keep your opinions to yourself."

Bonnie caught Libby's eye and shook her head at her. "We'll support any decision you make, Gwenny. We know this must be hard on you."

Gwen took gulping breaths, trying to calm her temper. She had supper on the stove for Walt. It was just a beef stew, but she happened to know it was one of his favorite meals. "I'll be at your house as soon as I've finished the supper dishes, Bonnie. I won't be sleeping with the man until this is settled."

Bonnie nodded. "All right."

Chapter Eight

Gwen's sisters cleared out an hour before the men were due home. There was no doubt in her mind why they'd left earlier than usual. They didn't want to be there to witness their sister's bad behavior. She didn't blame them. There *would* be bad behavior.

When Walt came in she smiled at him sweetly. "Did you have a good day?" she asked, getting up to serve his dinner.

"It was good. We're missing Bart's hands, but it's going well." He washed his hands and took his seat at the table. "Dinner smells good."

She put a bowl of stew on the table in front of him. "Would you like water or milk with dinner tonight?" She carefully kept her voice soft and sweet, not letting a bit of her anger show through.

"Milk sounds good." He leaned in and sniffed deeply. "Your cooking gets better every day."

She was hoping he'd say that. She filled a glass with milk and walked to the table, dumping the entire glass over his head. She moved away from him, not certain how he'd react.

Walt jumped up sputtering. "What's gotten into you?" He wiped the milk from his face with the napkin she'd placed on the table for him.

"Into me? Why, not a thing." She folded her arms across her chest, glaring at him. "Your mistress was here today. She's expecting. Did you know?"

Walt stared at her in surprise. "My mistress? I don't have a mistress." While

Walt had taken women to his bed over the years, there had never been one he'd kept for any period of time.

Gwen nodded, absolutely furious with him for pretending not to know who she was talking about. "Lela Mason. You do remember Lela, don't you, dear?"

Walt frowned for a moment as he thought about it. There'd been a Lela in a saloon in St. Louis, but he hadn't seen her in ages, and he'd never had relations with her. "Sure, I remember Lela, but she's not expecting my baby."

Gwen picked up the object closest to her which happened to be the wooden spoon she'd used for stirring the stew. It went flying at him, missing his ear by inches, but only because he'd ducked quickly. "Don't lie to me, Walton Dalton!"

Walt strode toward her, getting angrier by

the second. She was taking the word of a whore over his? "I'm not lying to you. You need to settle down, Gertie."

Gwen froze. Whether he was lying to her or not, she was in love with a man who didn't even know her first name. What was wrong with her? Very softly, she said, "My name is Gwen." She walked into the bedroom and picked up the carpet bag she'd packed and walked to the door. "I'll be staying at Bonnie's for a while."

Walt stood and watched her leave, kicking his chair. "Gwen. Why can't I ever remember that her name is Gwen?" What was he going to do? His wife had just left him. He sat down and calmly ate his stew, his mind working the whole while. He'd have to find Lela and force her to tell Gertie, er *Gwen*, the truth. How could his marriage have gone from nearly perfect to awful in less than twenty-four hours?

*****

Gwen rapped softly on Bonnie's door, waiting patiently until her sister opened the door.

As soon as Bonnie opened the door, Gwen walked in, calmly set her things on her sisters table, and threw herself into her sister's arms.

Bonnie held Gwen tightly. "It's going to be all right."

Gwen pulled away, wiping her nose inelegantly. "He doesn't deny knowing her. He says the baby isn't his, though." Why would he admit to only part of it if it wasn't the truth?

"Do you believe him?"

Gwen shrugged. "I think so. I'm not sure. If he was going to lie to me, wouldn't he have lied about knowing her as well?"

Bonnie nodded. "Probably. Why did you leave then?"

"He called me Gertie!" Gwen still couldn't believe she was in love with a man who didn't even know her name. How could he not know her name after a whole week of marriage? And of all names to call her, Gertie was the biggest insult he could have come up with.

Bonnie sighed. "He still doesn't know your name?" She shook her head. "Do you think leaving him will teach him your name?"

"Well, I didn't really leave him. I'm just taking a break from living with him. I'll go over and fix his breakfast in the morning." Gwen had thought it all out. She'd cook his meals, but she wouldn't make herself available to him sexually until everything was settled.

"I'm not sure you're doing the best thing, Gwenny. You need to give him another chance."

"Another chance to learn my name? He'll get a chance, but he needs to get everything squared away with Miss Mason and figure my name out first. I'm not messing around anymore." Gwen looked around at Bonnie's house. "Can I sleep with you?"

"Of course. Bart's gone, so it only makes sense you share my bed. I'm not sure if you can stay after he gets back, though." Bonnie bit her lip, unsure of how to handle things.

"That's fine. I'm sure Walt will get everything settled within a day or two." At least Gwen hoped he would. She didn't want to be without him any more than he wanted to be without her.

"If you say so." Bonnie fussed over her sister helping her get settled in for the night.

"I bet you never thought we'd be living together again." Gwen changed into her nightgown and took out her brush. Her waist-length hair took time to brush every night. "While I'm here, how would you like me to help you find a more flattering hairstyle?"

Bonnie looked at her with surprise. "What's wrong with my hairstyle?"

"Nothing. I just thought you'd like something different. I'm sure that Bart would like to see your hair done differently from time to time."

"I'll think on it."

*****

True to her word, Gwen was up before dawn, hurrying to her own cabin in the cold morning air. She was shivering as she squatted before the stove, starting the fire.

She went down to the cellar and selected a ham to cut into pieces and fry up for breakfast to go with the pancakes she was fixing.

Walt was startled to see Gwen at the stove when he got up to milk the cows. Between the three brothers, they had three cows. They took turns milking them, and today was his day. He would divide the milk three ways and deliver the other two pails to his brothers' homes.

"Good morning, Gwen." Walt made sure he spoke her name clearly, so she'd know he'd learned his lesson about her name.

"Good morning. Breakfast will be ready soon. You'd best hurry with the milking."

Walt sighed. Her voice had been colder than a winter morning. He'd make it up to her, though. He walked to the barn that housed their cows, going straight to the milking stool. The steady sounds of the milk hitting the pail always soothed him. The sounds reminded him of his childhood, when he and his brothers had been responsible for milking the cows every morning. It had been no easy task to milk every cow on the family's dairy farm, but now he missed it.

When he was finished, he delivered the buckets to Libby and then to Bonnie. When the latter answered her door, he asked, "What should I do? How can I win her back?"

Bonnie sighed. "You need to go talk with Miss Mason and have her tell Gwen the truth. She believes you. She's mainly angry that you didn't know her name now."

Walt looked down. "I should have shown her that I value her more than I have. Why on earth didn't I know my own wife's name?"

"I have no idea. You do now, though? That's what really matters."

Walt nodded. "I do. I'm going to try to

talk to her over breakfast."

Bonnie bit her lip for a moment, as if she was debating what to say to Walt. Finally, she said, "With Gwen you need to give her time to get over her mad. Act like nothing happened. Don't bring her flowers. Don't apologize. She'll just make you grovel. Instead, treat her like you always have. If she turns away from you, then so be it. She needs Miss Mason to tell her the truth, though. That's the only thing you can do."

"Thank you."

Bonnie's gaze turned cold and hard, setting the hairs on the back of his neck on end. "Don't hurt her again," was all she said, but Walt wasn't stupid. He knew there was an 'or else' hidden in her message. It was silly to be afraid of such a tiny woman, but in that moment, he felt real fear.

*****

Walt left immediately after breakfast. "I won't be on the ranch today. I need to go into town. Do you need anything?"

Gwen shook her head. "We have all the supplies we need." She kept her back to him as she washed up the breakfast dishes. She knew her sisters would be there any moment, and she was glad. She needed to talk to them.

Once the three of them were sitting together working on the curtains for Bonnie's house once again, Gwen asked, "Do you think I'm being too harsh? I don't want to be unreasonable, but he thought my name was Gertie!"

Bonnie shrugged. "I don't think you're being harsh exactly, but I think if you want to have a happy marriage, you need to forgive him. He knows your name now, doesn't he?"

Gwen nodded, a frown on her face. "Shouldn't he have known my name all along, though? I mean, I know his name!"

"Yes, he should have known it," Libby said. "But he's human. He still calls me Lizzy. I think he just has trouble with names."

"It's a strange thing to have trouble with!" Gwen protested, but she remembered that she had wished she could find a flaw in her mostly-perfect husband. Maybe this was his biggest flaw. If so, was it really so bad?

Libby shrugged. "Everyone has their quirks."

"So you think I should forgive him? Both of you?"

Bonnie nodded. "I do. I think you care for him, and I know he cares for you. There's no reason to hold a grudge."

"Forgive him, Gwen. He's a good man.

Why would you allow your marriage to suffer for a simple mistake?" Libby added.

"A man not knowing his own wife's name after a week of marriage is not a simple mistake. But all right. I'll think on it some more."

The sisters were baking a cake when they heard horses out front again. Gwen threw the door open without looking this time, knowing it would be Lela Mason once again. "What do you want?" she asked rudely.

Lela slowly climbed down from her seat behind the horse. "I came to tell you I lied to you. Walton was the kindest man who ever came into the saloon where I worked. I hoped I could come here, and he'd marry me just to help me out. When I realized he was married, I should have just left, but I had built it up so far in my head that I was certain he needed to help me. I'm sorry."

Gwen frowned. "So he's not the father?"

Lela shook her head. "Walt never needed to pay for the girls in the saloon. We all wished he would, but he never did." A tear escaped her eye. "I got fired as soon as the owner of the saloon I worked in found out I was expecting. I just needed somewhere to go."

"You drove all the way to Texas hoping he'd marry you?" Gwen shook her head. Walt sure did make an impression on people.

"I took a train. I have money saved up. It's not much, but it was enough for a train ticket and some money for living expenses." Lela shook her head. "I need to figure out what I'm going to do. I don't want to be living my old lifestyle with a baby."

Gwen's heart went out to the other woman. "I don't blame you for that at all. You should go to church with us on Sunday.

I'm sure one of the cowboys would be happy to marry you, even knowing your, err, colorful past."

Lela laughed. "I'm not sure that colorful is the word you're looking for, Mrs. Dalton."

Walt rode up on his horse and dismounted. He eyed Gwen warily. The last time she'd talked to Lela she'd dumped milk over his head. "Is everything settled?"

Gwen nodded slowly. She did love him, and forgiving him was the Christian thing to do. "I think so."

He walked to her and hugged her close. "You'll come home to me, Gwen?" He used her name deliberately, so she'd know he hadn't forgotten.

"Yes, I will. I'll get my bag from Bonnie's before supper." It was already late afternoon. The trip to Weatherford was a long one, though it was shorter on horseback than it was in a wagon. She smiled up at him. "Thank you for finally learning my name."

He shook his head. "I've always been terrible with names. I should have learned yours weeks ago."

"Yes, you really should have. I forgive you, though." She looked over his shoulder at Lela. "Won't you stay for tea, Miss Mason?"

Lela looked startled. "I'd be happy to."

Walt pulled away and pulled a letter from his pocket. "A letter for you from a Miss Edna Blue. I take it she's kin?"

Gwen took the letter from him with a smile. "She's my aunt." Gwen had never actually met her Aunt Edna, but they'd struck up a correspondence years ago when her father had been complaining about his eccentric sister. Gwen had thought she sounded fun, so she had written to her. "Thank you."

Walt nodded. "Will you make me a sandwich? I've lost half a day of work already, and I'd rather eat out on the range."

"I'd be happy to." Gwen hurried into the house and fixed him two bacon sandwiches, which she wrapped in paper. She came back out with them, seeing her sisters talking to Lela as if she were an old friend. They really did need to find her a husband. But who did they know who wouldn't mind marrying a former woman of the night?

After Walt rode off, Gwen looked at Bonnie. "Would you fix lunch for us all? I want to read Aunt Edna's letter."

"Yes, of course." Bonnie hurried to the stove to cook lunch while Libby stayed outside to talk to Lela.

Gwen went into the house and sat at the table, opening her letter with glee. Aunt Edna's letter were always a joy to read.

"My dear Gwen,

I'm happy to hear you're safe and in a better situation now. My brother needs some help when it comes to parenting, I see. He should never have locked you in your room. What utter nonsense that a rumor was started about you, and you were punished for it. That tramp Gertie needs to have a switch taken to her bottom.

So you're a married woman now? I think that's wonderful. I almost married once, but alas, my one true love died. I'm certain it was my fault. You see, we were in the woods one afternoon about a month before the wedding, and we had decided we were tired of waiting. So there I was, lying naked in his arms, and he had a heart attack right on top of me! Never fear, though. I'm still a virgin. We didn't have time to complete the act before he died. How I wish we had. I'm certain it was

God's way of punishing me for agreeing to do something I oughtn't.

You'll need to let me know what you think of Texas. I'd love to come to visit you sometime, once the first bloom of love has worn off. No one needs to hear the sounds newlyweds make during the night.

Your husband's name is Walton Dalton? That's terribly unfortunate. I do hope you can talk him into just using his initials or something. No woman should be forced to have a husband named Walton Dalton. Who would do that to a child, I ask you?

My life is the same as always. Day in and day out I make hats. Ever since Papa died life has been so lonely. Maybe someday things will change. I hope to retire soon and see the world. I'm almost sixty years old now. If I'm going to do it, I need to do it soon.

All my love,

Edna"

Gwen found herself chuckling repeatedly as she read the missive. She hoped to meet Aunt Edna in person sometime soon. Maybe when her aunt retired, she would make the trip to Texas to see them. She'd be welcomed with open arms.

Chapter Nine

Lela was handy with a needle, so the sisters put her to work helping make the curtains that afternoon. They talked while they worked, trying to come up with an idea to help Lela.

"Maybe you could start a sewing business?" Libby suggested. "With as many bachelors as there are around here, I'm sure someone to do their mending and make clothes for them would be welcome."

Lela thought about it for a moment. "You know, that's really not a bad idea. I enjoy sewing, and I would be able to have my baby with me all the time."

"You'd have time to meet the men around here and decide which one suits your fancy if any. There are some men at church who seem nice enough," Gwen added.

"Just make sure you're honest with whomever you choose," Bonnie said. "I'd hate for a man to marry you only to be upset that you once had a less than desirable lifestyle."

Lela laughed. "You girls sure have some interesting ways of avoiding saying I was a whore."

All three sisters blushed at Lela's candidness. None of them had ever been around anyone who spoke that way. Gwen suddenly let out a giggle.

"What's wrong with you, Gwen?" Libby asked.

"Oh, I was just thinking about how Mama would react if she knew we'd run away to Texas and were sitting in my new house entertaining a *former* whore."

Bonnie covered her mouth with her hand as she started giggling too. "She'd have an apoplectic fit!"

Libby shook her head. "We'd be hauled back to Massachusetts and forced to marry those lecherous old men for certain."

Lela looked between them. "Forced to marry lecherous old men?"

Bonnie quickly told the story that had brought them to Texas, conveniently leaving out the scandal and Gwen's incarceration.

Gwen looked at her sister admiringly. She'd told enough of the story that the other woman would understand without going into details that Gwen didn't want known. She was amazed at her sister's skill with words.

Lela shook her head. "That's awful. No young lady should ever have to marry a lecherous old man." She shuddered. "I've had enough of them touching me that I wouldn't wish it on anyone."

Gwen frowned. "Would you tell us how you happened upon your former vocation? If the question's not too personal, of course."

All three sisters watched Lela. They probably wouldn't have the opportunity to speak with a former prostitute this way ever again, so they were going to make the most of it.

Lela obviously loved having an audience. "Well, it started out simply. I was an orphan and put on an orphan train headed West in 1869. I was only twelve at the time. When I got off the train with the other orphans in St. Louis, I was chosen by a couple who hadn't been able to have children of their own. The woman was wonderful to me and became the mother I'd always dreamed of having. The man...he was something else entirely. He came to my bed every night and forced himself on me." She shook her head. "I left when I was sixteen. I was certain I would be able to find work doing something respectable. I was wrong. Within two months I was starving, and I walked past a saloon. The bartender took one look at me and asked if I needed work. I said 'yes' immediately, because any work was better than starving. I didn't know what he wanted me to do until I got my first customer. I always knew I'd get out, though. I started saving from that first night. I worked there for over ten years, saving every single dime I made. I knew I'd either get too old to work there or something would happen."

"I just can't imagine," Gwen said. "Did it bother you?"

"Of course it did. I spent the first twelve years of my life in an orphanage run by the good Catholic sisters. I believed that enjoying relations with my husband was wrong, and I was having relations with several men every night. I felt, and still feel, like I'm going to burn in hell. But what choice did I have?" A tear drifted down Lela's cheek, but she brushed it away. "I am what I am. I did what I did. I can't change any of it."

Gwen shook her head. "No, you really can't." She reached out and took Lela's hand in hers. "You don't have to go back to that, you know. We'll help you set up a seamstress shop. There's got to be a place in Wiggieville for you to live."

"Wiggieville? I've been staying in Weatherford."

"Wiggieville is a small town only an hour's drive from here. We'll find someone who will let you board with them. Maybe you can sell shirts out of the mercantile there. The owner is really nice." Bonnie leaned forward excitedly as she made the suggestion.

"Yes, we need to find you a place in Wiggieville," Libby agreed. "We can meet you there tomorrow morning and help you get settled if you'd like."

Lela tilted her head to one side. "I think that's a really good idea. Yes, let's do it. Then I can accept a man or not. Whatever I want to do. Will people buy clothes from a whore though?"

"Former whore," Gwen reminded her. "I don't see why you have to tell everyone you were a whore. Just say the father of the baby is no longer with us. He's not. He couldn't possibly be in Texas, could he?"

Lela laughed. "I like the way you think, Mrs. Dalton." She got to her feet, putting the finished curtain on the table. "I need to head back to town. I don't want to be out driving alone after dark."

Gwen followed her out to her buggy, hugging her. "I never thought I'd count a former lady of the evening as one of my friends. I'm glad to be able to say I was wrong."

"So am I," Lela said, hugging her back. "I'll see you in town in the morning. Around nine?"

"Yes. I'm sure anyone can give you directions to Wiggieville." Gwen stepped back and looked at the horse and buggy. "Are these rented?"

"Yes, but I can drive them to Wiggieville. If I decide to move here, I'm certain it won't be a problem to get there after returning the horse."

"There's a stagecoach," Gwen told her.

"Oh good. That will make things simple then."

Gwen watched as the other woman

climbed nimbly into the buggy. She hoped she would be able to move so easily when she was six months pregnant. She raised her hand to wave goodbye as the other woman drove away. It was so nice to make new friends.

*****

Over dinner that evening, Gwen related what they'd decided to do to Walt.

Walt shook his head. "Are you serious? She came here, lied to you, caused a fight between us, and you're going to help her find work and settle in the area? Who does that?"

"I do apparently. She's such a nice lady that I hate the thought of her being alone and pregnant. I hope she can get enough work to sustain her and the baby once her savings run out."

"A nice lady. She's a whore!" Walton

couldn't believe his ears.

"No, she's not. She's a *former* whore. And she's my new friend, so I'll thank you not to speak of her that way."

"I'm not going to be able to convince you not to help her, am I?"

Gwen grinned at him. "No, you're not." She toyed with her potatoes for a moment. "Do you mind hitching up the wagon for us in the morning? I'd do it myself, but I don't know how."

"And if I refuse?"

She shrugged. "I'm not stupid. I can figure it out for myself."

For a moment, he sat staring at her stunned. Just a few weeks before she had been uncertain about how to get water from a well, and he'd had to show her. Now she was certain she could hitch up a team of horses on her own. "I'll do it," he said finally. "I don't know why you're so determined to help her, but I'll do it."

"Oh, thank you." She smiled her best smile, the one that had once had men begging for her affections.

Walt frowned. "You won't get around me that way, you know."

"Oh, I know that. I just like to smile at you." She reached across the table and took his hand in hers. "I'm sorry I dumped milk over your head."

"I thought I married this biddable young lady. I guess I was wrong."

"Oh, I've never been that. Young lady, yes. Biddable? My mother wishes I was."

*****

They found Lela a boarding house to live in the following morning. She didn't say what had happened to the baby's father and the tired looking woman who ran the house didn't ask. "It'll be an extra fifty cents a month once the baby is here."

The woman had introduced herself as Mrs. Rogers. She said she was a widow, and kept a clean home. She was in her mid-fifties with gray hair and sad brown eyes. Gwen's heart went out to her automatically.

Lela nodded. "That shouldn't be a problem. I'm looking to start doing some sewing for folks in the area. Would you know of anyone who needs that kind of help?"

"Oh, plenty round here need help with sewing and mending. We'll make up a letter to post on the bulletin board at the mercantile. You'll have more work than you can handle in no time."

"Oh, thank you, Mrs. Rogers." Lela looked at Gwen. "I'll be back later tonight or first thing tomorrow. I have to see when the stagecoach runs."

"That sounds just fine. Just let me know when you get back and I'll give you a key."

As they left, Lela was practically dancing. "It's going to work!"

Gwen smiled. "Our plans always work," she said. She and her sisters had come up with more than their share of plans over the years. Of course none of them had been to help a former-prostitute.

"Thank you. All of you! I can't believe I'm finally going to be respectable."

Gwen hugged Lela goodbye. "We'll see you at church on Sunday, right?"

"Oh, I don't know about that," Lela told her. "I'd be afraid that the church would be struck by lightning. I wouldn't want to be responsible for all those deaths."

Bonnie smiled. "Don't you worry about

that. Jesus ministered to prostitutes."

"You girls help me look at things so differently. Thanks again," she said as she climbed into her buggy. "I'll see you on Sunday, but if the church burns down it's your fault not mine."

"We'll happily take the blame," Libby said with a grin.

They went to the mercantile to mail the letter Gwen had written to Aunt Edna before heading back to the ranch. "Thanksgiving is coming up," Bonnie said. "Are you all right with hosting that, Libby?"

"I'll make the mashed potatoes," Gwen offered.

"I'll make the turkey," Bonnie replied. "If Bart's home in time to kill one for me that is."

"When do you expect him back?" Gwen asked.

Bonnie shrugged. "He wasn't certain.

Soon, I hope."

Gwen was glad that it was Bart's job to go on the business trips and not Walt's. She'd have hated having to give her husband up so often. Bonnie didn't seem to like it, but she handled it better than Gwen would have.

Chapter Ten

Gwen and her sisters had been in Texas for about two months when she realized something was wrong. She and her sisters had always had their monthlies together, and she hadn't had one since they'd been there while her sisters had bled twice. The first time, she hadn't been terribly concerned about. When it happened again, she decided to talk to Bonnie about it.

Bart was off on another business trip, so she went over immediately after breakfast. The sisters still got together every afternoon, but they no longer needed as much instruction, so they all tended to stay home and do their own housework in the mornings.

She knocked on the door and waited

patiently, shivering slightly. It was chilly, not cold enough for snow, but she should have brought her shawl.

Bonnie opened the door wide. "What's wrong, Gwen?"

Gwen sighed, taking a seat at the table. "I'm really not sure, but something is. I haven't had a cycle since we've come to Texas, and the new dress you made me doesn't fit any longer. The old ones do, but that's because I lost so much weight before we left home."

Bonnie smiled. "Gwenny, don't you know that women miss their cycles when they're carrying?"

Gwen stared at her sister for a moment before swallowing hard. "You mean...You think I'm going to have a baby?" The only pregnant woman she'd ever been around was Lela, and they hadn't talked about things of a personal nature. She found that when Lela started talking, she said way too much for her.

"I do." Bonnie pulled up the other chair and sat beside her sister, reaching out to take hold of her hand. "I'm so happy for you!"

Gwen sat back, stunned beyond belief. Yes, she'd known that she could get pregnant now that she was married, but she hadn't thought too much about it. She'd been too busy trying to learn to cook and keep the house properly. Did she even want a baby yet?

Bonnie laughed. "Don't look so shocked. You knew a baby could come of your time with Walt. I told you it could when I explained about the marriage bed."

"I thought it would take longer," Gwen said helplessly. "I'm going to have a baby." She put her hand over her stomach trying to absorb the fact that she was actually carrying another person inside her. "I don't know how to take care of a baby!"

"Libby and I will help you. You'll be fine."

"I need to tell Walt." What would he say? Did he even want a baby? He kept talking about building an empire, so she thought he did, but she just wasn't certain.

"Why don't you make him a nice meal? You can tell him over dessert. What's his favorite dessert?"

Gwen shrugged. "If it's sweet, Walt loves it. That man has a sweet tooth like I've never seen."

"Okay, so we'll bake a cake, and you can tell him while you eat it. He'll be happy. Don't worry."

Gwen got up and walked toward the door. She had chores to do. "When do I need to see a doctor?" she asked.

Bonnie shook her head. "I don't think there are any doctors close by. We'll find you a good midwife."

"A baby," Gwen said under her breath as she opened the door and walked toward home. She was going to have a baby.

*****

Gwen made a pot roast for dinner and a cake with whipped cream for dessert. Walt seemed to be partial to whipped cream, so she used that instead of making icing.

Walt's face lit up when she brought the cake out. "That looks great. Are we celebrating something special?"

Walt asked her the same thing every time she baked a cake. "We're celebrating the fact that I baked a cake today."

He laughed softly as she put a piece in

front of him. He took a bite and closed his eyes, savoring the flavor. "This is amazing. Did you do something different?"

"I put whipped cream on it. I thought you'd like it better that way." Gwen walked around the table and took her spot across from him. Gwen had thought all day about how she would tell him about the baby. She wanted it to be just right. "You know that empire you keep talking about building?"

Walt nodded. "We're well on our way!"

Gwen smiled. "Our first little subject is on its way too." She ate just a bite of the whipped cream, watching his face carefully.

"Our first subject?" Walt stopped eating with his fork poised in mid-air. "What does that mean?"

Gwen patted her belly with a smile. "Our first subject will be here in a few months. Bonnie said about seven or so."

Walt's eyes grew wide. "You mean...we're having a baby?"

Gwen nodded, her whole face lit up. "Yes, a baby. Are you happy?"

"Of course I am! I can't wait until I can hold him in my arms."

"What if he's a she?" Gwen didn't really care about the gender of the baby, but she had to tease him.

"Then I can't wait to hold her in my arms." He walked around the table, took her hand and pulled her to her feet. His cake was forgotten. He hugged her tight and then looked her up and down. "I can see where you've gained a little weight. Your face is fuller."

She made a face. What woman wanted to be told she'd gained weight, even if it was because she was carrying? "Part of that is gaining back the weight I lost while I was locked in my room for two months," she told him without thinking.

Walt's face changed, a fire coming into his eyes. "You were locked in your room for two months?"

Gwen bit her lip. She hadn't meant to tell him that. He didn't know about the scandal. "It was nothing."

"You were locked in your room for two months, lost weight as a result, and it was nothing? I need to hear this story, Gwen. Don't make me take a train all the way to Massachusetts to strangle your parents." Why hadn't she told him about being locked in her room before?

Gwen sighed. "It's a long story. Finish your cake while I tell you." Talking about what had happened just before she left Beckham was not something she'd ever expected to do with him.

He gave her a look that told her he wasn't going to give in before walking around the table and picking up his fork. "I'm eating. Talk to me."

She took her time sitting back down, taking a sip of her milk before starting the story. "When I went to school there was this girl I knew. Her name was Gertie, and she hated me. No one has ever hated me the way Gertie did. We were rivals for everything. If someone was Gertie's friend, they couldn't be my friend, and the opposite was true as well."

Walton nodded as he continued eating his cake. He'd hear the whole story out before he said anything.

"My last year of school I was courted by a young man in our class named Stanley. He was nice enough, but I realized he wasn't the man I wanted to spend my life with so I ended things between us." Really? She'd moved on

232

to older men at that point, but she didn't want to tell her husband that. "Gertie started stepping out with Stanley soon after that. They've been a couple for three years now, and were married not long before we left Beckham.

"I got a note in late June from Gertie asking me if we could iron out our differences. She asked me to meet her in a local park. I wasn't sure why Gertie wanted to make amends when we'd never gotten along, but I went to meet her. I didn't like having someone hate me the way Gertie always had.

"When I reached the park, Gertie wasn't there. It was Stanley. He told me he missed me, and that he realized Gertie wasn't the woman for him. He asked if I would consider a relationship with him. I told him I wasn't interested, and he needed to not contact me again. When I started to leave, he grabbed my arm and kissed me, so I stomped on his foot and ran home."

Walt waited for the rest of the story, but when it wasn't forthcoming he asked, "And you were locked in your room because?"

Gwen sighed. "Gertie found out about the kiss somehow. So she spread a rumor that I was expecting, and that my sisters and I had all kissed the same man. It wasn't true, but my parents decided it was time to 'take me in hand.' They locked me in my room while my father found a man who would be willing to marry me." She shuddered then, a single tear rolling down her cheek. "They found the most despicable man I know. He was a deacon of our church, and he always looked at me like he wanted to eat me for breakfast. He was in his forties and much too old for me. They agreed that Bonnie and Libby would also marry, because they were part of the scandal as well. They were supposed to marry two other deacons of the church, who were of a similar age and mindset."

"So you refused to marry the men and came here instead?"

Gwen shook her head. "I spent two months in my room. I refused to eat for a while and lost weight. My sisters are the ones who agreed to the marriages. They came to my room and liberated me in the middle of the night. We had to sneak out of the house and to the train station. Our parents don't know where we are.

"Bonnie didn't even tell me where we were going. She said we were going to visit her school friend, Anna, who lives in Wiggieville. Instead, we ended up here. You and Nate were waiting for our train."

Walt stared at her in surprise. "Why

didn't you tell me?" He believed that she'd been innocent of wrongdoing. Well, mostly innocent. There was no doubt in his mind that she'd played with the affections of the men back in Beckham like she'd tried to play with his when she'd first arrived. What angered him was that she'd hidden it from him.

"I didn't want you to be angry with me. I wasn't certain you'd even want to be married to me if you knew I'd been involved in a scandal back home." She watched his face to see if it made him hate her.

Walt shook his head. "Gwen, I don't love you for who you were in the past. Obviously not. You were a selfish child. I love the woman you've become. The strong woman who will help a whore who lied to you."

"Former whore," she corrected automatically. "Wait. You love me?" He'd never said the words to her before.

"Of course, I love you. How could I help but? You're a good woman with a huge capacity to love." Walt sighed. "I don't like that you didn't tell me the truth about this, though."

Gwen frowned. "I know. I won't hide things from you anymore. I promise."

Walt nodded. "I hope not. There's nothing we can do but go on, I guess." He shook his head. "You were giving me joyful news tonight. Let's not mar the memory of our special evening."

Gwen stood and started clearing the table, hoping she hadn't ruined things by telling him the truth. Never had she loved anyone the way she loved Walt.

Once the dishes were done, he stood and took her into his arms, holding her tightly. "I'm thrilled about the baby. He will someday be the emperor of our huge ranch."

"Wouldn't that make him the rancher, not the emperor?" she asked with a grin.

He leaned down and kissed her softly. "Whatever his title, he'll be our son. Someday, the Dalton name will be a legend in this part of Texas. And you, Gwen? You'll be the woman who made it all happen. The empress by my side." He kissed her forehead, stroking his hands up and down her arms. "When I sent for a mail order bride, I didn't expect to find love. I expected companionship and a hard-working wife who would help me build my empire. Instead, I got the woman I will cherish for the rest of my days."

Gwen leaned against him, her arms around him. "And I got the only man I will ever love. I hope the others are as happy as we are."

Epilogue

The Dalton Ranch, Christmas Day, 1888

Gwen sat at the table for Christmas dinner, looking at her loved ones around her. It was hard to believe three of the people that had become some of the most important in her life had been strangers to her less than three months before.

"That was a fine meal Libby, Gwen," Nate told them with a nod as he patted his stomach. "I don't know when I've eaten as much."

"And to think we had no help from Bonnie!" Gwen was thrilled to say she and Libby had cooked the whole meal themselves. Bonnie still helped them with a lot of things, and she'd had a lot to do with the planning, but she hadn't helped. Not one little bit.

Walt kissed her on the cheek. "You're a wonderful cook. I can't wait for you to teach our ...well, whatever it is we're having." He truly didn't care if he had a boy or a girl, just so the baby was healthy, and Gwen had an easy time carrying it.

"Even if it's a boy?" asked Bart.

"Even if it's a boy," Walt responded, smiling. He believed that boys should be able to cook as well as girls.

"Who's ready for dessert?" Bonnie asked, seeming uncomfortable with the conversation.

"You know I am!" said Walt and Bart together.

All six of them burst into laughter. They laughed so hard, no one noticed when the door was thrown open.

Walt jumped to his feet. "What the..." He stilled at the sound of shotguns being cocked. Who could possibly be interrupting their Christmas dinner with threats against them?

Three men stood just inside Nate and Libby's cabin, looking very angry. But not as angry as Gwen. "Benedict! What are you doing here?" What on God's green earth did her brothers think they were going to do with those guns pointed at her husband and brothers-in-law?

Walt looked back and forth between the only man looking at his wife and Gwen. What connection did the two of them have?

Bonnie looked astonished. "Hank?"

Bart narrowed his eyes threateningly at the man in the middle before turning to Bonnie. "Who the hel…"

"Percy?" Libby's face turned pale as she stared at the newcomers.

The Dalton brothers looked at each other. None of them had guns, and the strangers were obviously known to their wives. What could they do? Walt tried to think quickly, used to getting out of bad situations with his wits.

"Get em up," snarled Benedict. "Now!"

The Dalton brothers knew there was no way to fight without weapons, so they all slowly raised their hands in the air.

"Gwen, Libby, Bonnie, get over here. We're... taking you home." The one in the middle, the best looking of the three, gave the order.

Bonnie stood, staring at the man. "Hank? What in heaven's name are you doing here?"

"We might ask you the same question!" insisted the one Libby had called Percy.

"If you must know, we live here!" Gwen all but rolled her eyes at her brothers. Why were they in Texas? They belonged in Massachusetts. Didn't they

243

realize they weren't welcome?

"Yes, we can see that." Benedict took a step forward, trying to look menacing. "And it looks mighty cozy."

"You can't take us back! You just can't!" Libby sounded like she was about to cry, and Gwen wanted to tell her to hush. They needed to keep their wits about them if they were going to get rid of their brothers so they stay in Texas, building the empire Walt kept insisting on.

"Take you back?" Nate said, his hands, still held in the air were balled into fists. "What are you talking about? Who are these men?"

"We'd like to know the same about you!" Percy raised his shotgun.

"I don't care who you are! You're

trespassing, get off our land!" Walt looked like he was willing to take on all three of the men in front of him with his bare hands.

"You're hardly in a position to demand anything," Hank said. "All we want are these women."

"Yeah, they've caused us a lot of trouble the last few months!" Benedict looked furious.

"How could we?" asked Gwen. "We've been here the whole time!" They couldn't blame her for more problems back home. It had been bad enough to be blamed when Gertie started a rumor about her, but to be blamed for God knows what when she hadn't even been in the state? No, she would *not* accept that at all.

"Precisely. Which is why we've come to fetch you and take you back to where and whom you belong," Percy aimed his gun at Nate's heart.

"Percy! Don't!" Libby cried.

"Don't what? Shoot this scum for running off with ya? Or was it the other way around?" Percy looked back and forth between Libby and Nate, as if he was trying to figure out exactly how his sisters had ended up in the brothers' care.

Bonnie had obviously had it with all the bickering back and forth. "Enough!"

"Bonnie, please," Hank warned. "We *have* to do this."

"Shut up, all of you!" Bart shouted.

"I say we hang these scum!" Percy yelled.

All three sisters were now on their feet. "No!"

Gwen tried to get between Walt and her brothers, knowing they wouldn't harm her, but Walt pushed her behind him, knocking her to the floor. She let out a sob. She couldn't let anything happen to the baby. She wanted to jump up and get between them, but what if she was knocked down again? She had to think of the baby first!

How had their brothers found them in Texas? Hank had helped them escape, but had he known exactly where they were going? Had he betrayed them? Bonnie trusted him, but was it smart?

She listened to the fight going on around them, hoping no one would be hurt. She was more worried about Walt than anyone, but could she ever forgive him if he killed one of her brothers? She bowed her head and prayed harder than she'd ever prayed. "Please God, don't let anyone get hurt. Please let all of them stay safe. I don't want to go home with my brothers, but I don't want them dead either. Please God, only You can see a way to keep them all safe."

Gwen could hear scuffling and the sounds of fist on flesh. She kept her eyes closed, afraid of who could be getting hurt.

"Sit down, all of you!" Bonnie demanded.

Gwen opened her eyes. Why was

Bonnie giving orders? What had happened? She poked her head out to see Bonnie holding a gun. Amazingly enough, she was now the only person holding a gun.

"Put that gun away before you shoot somebody!" Benedict tried to grab the gun from her.

"That's a good idea, maybe I oughta." Bonnie swung the gun barrel toward her brother.

Benedict's hands went up, as did Walt's. Neither of them seemed to trust a woman with a gun.

Gwen looked up and wanted to laugh. "Walt! She's not going to shoot you!" Didn't he realize she and her sisters wanted to stay in Texas? Poor Walt must not think a gun belonged in a woman's hands. She agreed with him, but she'd never tell Bonnie that. If anything could make her sister shoot her, that would be it...

Walt rubbed a lump on his head, shook it before pulling Gwen into his arms, kissing her softly on the forehead. Those buffoons better not have hurt his wife or his child. "Who are you?" He fairly barked out the words, angry beyond belief.

"We're the Blue brothers," said Hank. "And we've come to take our sisters home."

"Brothers?" asked Nate. He grabbed Libby to him. "You never said you had brothers."

"And our sisters never said they were leaving," added Percy.

"Leaving?" Bart asked. "What do ya mean, leaving?" He scowled at the three brothers in front of him.

"He means our sisters ran out on a scandal caused by Gwen," Benedict glared at his middle sister. "To alleviate any further damage to the family name, our father painstakingly chose a husband for each of them."

"Yeah, and how do they show their appreciation?" Percy looked angrier than the other two combined. "By running away! Pa sent us here to bring you back. Deacons Smith, Jackson, and Belafonte paid a tidy sum for us to do it, too."

"But you can't take us back!" Gwen didn't care what they did. She was not going back to that town where everyone thought she was a tramp. She wasn't.

"And why not?" asked Benedict moving toward Bonnie.

"Because we're all married, that's why!" Bonnie raised the gun higher.

Benedict stopped. "We figured that might happen, but Deacons Smith, Jackson, and Belafonte don't care. They want you three like fleas want a dog." The look on his face told Gwen that he couldn't figure out why anyone would want his sisters.

Libby and Gwen gasped. "If you're thinking that we're getting annulments you're sadly mistaken." Even if she weren't carrying, Gwen would never get her marriage annulled. For one reason, she didn't need another scandal in her life. For another? She happened to love her husband.

"It's been done before," said Percy. "I just hope these scum haven't dishonored you beyond repair."

Gwen shook her head. "They've done nothing of the sort. In fact, I'm not only married, I'm expecting!" She said the words proudly, waiting for her brothers to react.

All three of the Blue Brothers' eyes went to Gwen's belly. "You're lying," Benedict accused.

"No, I'm not," Gwen responded. She was so happy to be able to honestly tell him she was carrying. Even old man Belafonte wouldn't want her if she had some other man's baby growing in her body.

"So what if we only bring back two," asked Percy. "Two out of three isn't bad."

"Oh no you won't!" Libby folded her arms over her chest, standing her ground.

"And why not?" demanded Hank.

"Because ..." she looked up at Nate. "I'm going to have a baby too."

Nate blanched. "What? You are? Good God, Libby, are ya sure?"

"Yeah, are ya sure?" asked Benedict, who at this point looked even paler than Nate did.

"I'm sure," Libby said, putting her arms around Nate.

"Libby, my little Libby ..."

Walt looked at Gwen. If she'd known her sister was expecting, she'd certainly kept the secret from him. Gwen looked just as startled as he felt though, so he didn't think that was the case.

Percy's mouth opened in shock. "Looks like it's just you, Bonnie."

"I don't know what Deacon Smith paid you to bring us back, but I'm not going." Bonnie still held the gun, so it was clear she wasn't backing down.

"Put the gun down, Bonnie," Hank said, his voice low. "Let's talk about this. We... we can't go back empty handed." Hank held his hand out as if he expected her to hand him the gun.

"Why not?" Bonnie pointed the shotgun right at him.

"Because ..." Hank seemed to be nervous about something.

"Quiet!" snapped Percy. "Let's just take her and go."

"You're not taking my wife anywhere," Bart announced. "Bonnie, give me that gun." He held his hand out to his wife, waiting for her to give him her gun.

"No."

It was all Gwen could do not to giggle hysterically at the look of utter shock on Bart's face.

"What?" asked Bart.

"I said, no. These are our brothers, Bart, and they wouldn't be acting so desperate without a good reason." Bonnie held the gun steady.

"I'll not let them take you..." Bart sighed.

"You don't have to. I can't go either."

Bart took a step toward her. "Bonnie..."

"...because I'm expecting too."

"What?" Gwen and Libby cried in

unison. "Bonnie!"

Gwen couldn't believe her sisters had kept their pregnancies a secret from her. Why when they were next alone, she'd be giving them both a piece of her mind! She'd told everyone when she found out, and they had kept it all inside.

Suddenly a thought occurred to her. They'd better not have told each other without telling her. They'd kept their true purpose in Texas a secret from her. This had better not be another case of keeping things from Gwen!

"Bonnie?" Bart echoed, his face pale.

"So you see, my dear brothers, you've failed, as far as taking us back. Now the only question I have for you, is, what are you really doing here?" Bonnie didn't drop the gun as she waited on her brothers' reply.

*****

Gwen stood over Walton, searching his hair for the bump he kept complaining about. For such a big, strong man, he sure was complaining a lot about a little bump on top of his head. "You're going to be fine."

Walt wrapped his arms around her, holding her tightly. "Are you sure you're all right? I didn't mean to knock you down. I just wanted you to be safely behind me."

Gwen nodded. "I'm all right, and I'm not cramping. I'm pretty sure the baby is fine too. Good thing I landed on my backside isn't it?"

Walt laughed. "I happen to like your backside." He pulled her onto his lap and held her close. "I'm glad we were able to get rid of your brothers so easily. Do you think they'll head straight back to Massachusetts?"

Gwen shrugged. "I'm so mad at them right now, I really don't care what they do." She knew she wouldn't stay angry forever, but she certainly needed a break from Blue men for a while. A long while, she hoped.

"I'm so glad you're all right." He'd never been so frightened in his life as he'd been when her brothers had all stood there pointing guns at them. He wasn't afraid for himself, though. Only for Gwen and the baby. If he'd ever had an occasion to doubt his love for her, he didn't now. "I love you, sweetheart."

Gwen sighed happily. "And I love you, which is a good thing. Our empire needs strong leadership."

"Do you think they'll come back?" he asked.

She shook her head. "No, I don't. I think you scared them away with your threats to make certain they'd never father children if they came back with intentions of taking us."

She only hoped that someday, her brothers would be welcome in their little empire. They had heads as hard as rocks, but they would always be her brothers.

THE DRIFTER'S MAIL ORDER BRIDE

by

Cassie Hayes

Having grown up in the shadow of two beautiful sisters, 'Scrawny Bonnie' Blue knows she doesn't stand a chance at landing a good man in Beckham, Massachusetts. The only way she'll find a husband is by leaving her family behind to become a mail order bride. But when all three Blue sisters are swept up in a scandal, she has no choice to but to take 'Gorgeous Gwen' and 'Lovely Libby' with her…kicking and screaming, if she must.

Bart Dalton would be happy riding the

range forever, but his brothers need his help to start a ranch in north Texas. He figures he'll last a year or so before his feet get itchy again, which his brothers understand. As triplets, they can almost read each others' minds. Except when his oldest brother orders three brides for them all. It would have been nice to have a little warning about *that!*

When Bart is late to meet the train carrying the Blue sisters, his brothers get first dibs, leaving Bonnie standing alone and dejected once again. It only gets worse when her 'intended' finally shows up and balks at the idea of marrying her. The only thing Bonnie has going for her are her wits, and she puts them to good use by proposing a business arrangement that Bart can't refuse.

Will Bart go back to his drifter ways, or is the elusive thing he's been searching for all his life sleeping in the next room?

EXCERPT

The moment Bonnie and her sisters stepped off the train, she spotted two men who looked identical. The odds of there being a set of twins *and* a set of triplets meeting that particular train seemed low, so she assumed the third brother was simply out of sight.

Raising a tentative hand to the men, she started across the platform with Libby and a clueless Gwen, who was prattling on about the stagecoach ride they were supposed to be taking into Wiggieville to see Anne. The men met them halfway.

"Are you ladies the Blue sisters?" asked one of the men.

"Who are you?" Gwen said, as rude as ever.

"I'm Walton Dalton, and I pick you,"

replied the man. Then he did the most amazing thing. He pulled Gwen into a kiss — right there on the platform in front of God and everyone!

Gwen took care of him, though, by stomping on his foot, but he didn't seem deterred. In fact, he seemed more determined than ever, going so far as to say the preacher was standing by. And poor Gwen had no idea what was going on.

"Mr. Dalton," Bonnie said, addressing Walton and trying to keep the panic from her voice, "I'm Bonnie. I'm the oldest sister." He seemed completely nonplussed by this news so she elaborated further. "I believe I'm the one you're supposed to marry."

"I don't care who's oldest," he said, gazing down at Gwen. "I'm marrying this one."

He might just as well have punched

Bonnie in the stomach. She'd come all this way expecting to marry the eldest brother and who had he gone for? Gwen, of course. She shouldn't have been surprised, really, but it still stung.

"I believe your letter said there would be three of you," she managed to squeak out.

"That's my brother Nate," Walton said, nodding at his brother before flicking his eyes around the platform. "Bart should be here by now but I'm sure he'll be along."

Bonnie didn't really care about the inconsiderate brother Bart, who couldn't be bothered to keep an appointment. She had higher expectations from her future husband.

She turned to look at Nate but he couldn't seem to rip his gaze away from Libby, who was blushing furiously and peeking up at him from behind her dark lashes. This wouldn't do at all. She refused to be the consolation prize for the one who didn't show up on time.

"Libby's the youngest!" she fairly shouted, drawing surprised looks from everyone. Surely he would do the right thing and choose Bonnie over her baby sister. But of course Nate had been just as surprised as Gwen at the situation he'd found himself in and he simply looked confused.

To his credit, he adapted much more quickly than Gwen did, as soon as Walton explained, but Bonnie once again found herself ignored and rejected in favor of her prettier sisters. Bitterness settled over her heart at the realization her life would be no different outside of Beckham.

And now…now she was leftovers. The discarded garbage the other two brothers didn't want. She was table scraps! It was all she could do to choke back the tears as they waited for the tardy youngest brother.

What had she been thinking, bringing her sisters along? She'd registered with Elizabeth's mail order bride agency to leave Beckham — including her family — behind. With nothing to compare her to, her future husband might have been pleased with her. She was extremely skilled at homemaking and, when not standing next to her beautiful sisters, she wasn't altogether homely.

She'd ruined her entire life by putting the welfare of her sisters ahead of her own, just as she'd always done. Never once growing up had they shown her the same courtesy, so why did she feel so responsible for them? They certainly didn't refuse the advances of Walt and Nate, even though Bonnie made it very clear she expected to be the first chosen.

For five full minutes, she sat on that bench and hated her sisters. She wished and prayed for a runaway train to jump the tracks and barrel across the platform, taking them all with it. She would be the lone survivor, and the only person to turn up at the group funeral. Of course, she would be draped in black but behind her dark veil, she would be smiling. Maybe even laughing.

Then Libby reached over and squeezed her hand. The poor child was trembling. Bonnie's frozen heart melted, and she gave her youngest sister an encouraging smile. She couldn't begrudge either sister happiness, nor would she wish misery on them. And marrying those lecherous old deacons would have been a life sentence of misery.

Well, if she couldn't have love, she would at least do everything in her power to make sure her sisters were happy and cared for. If these two men, who were so entranced by their beauty, didn't do right by them, they'd have Bonnie to answer to.

As for her, she had little choice but to accept the errant Dalton as her husband. What little money they had left after the train journey wouldn't be enough for her to buy a meal, much less a ticket back home. The question was, would he accept her?

It looked like she was about to find out. Walton was striding across the platform to meet with a third man who looked just like him. As late as Bart was meeting them, Bonnie would have thought he'd have a little giddy-up in his get-along, but in fact he seemed quite unperturbed. Clearly the man was unreliable, inconsiderate and untrustworthy.

Wonderful.

Bonnie was just thinking that maybe marrying Deacon Smith would have been preferable to a layabout ne'er-do-well when Walt led his brother over to make introductions. Swallowing her pride — what was left of it, anyway — she stood and did her best to not glare at the man. Alienating him before he even found out they were to be married wouldn't help matters.

But the moment Bart's deeply tanned and calloused hand enveloped hers, the second his rich brown eyes met her own, all the words — every word she'd ever learned — flew right out of her head. A strange drumming roared in her ears, and she was surprised to discover it was her heart beating wildly. The palm he was holding so gently in his strong hand was suddenly wet with perspiration. Bonnie had never been left speechless in her life, and she didn't understand her strange reaction to this man.

But the spell was broken when Walt introduced her as Bart's bride. The look of sheer horror that flashed across his face was enough to bring her out of her stupor. Her brain was still trying to play catch-up but two words managed to rise to the surface. Two words that would show she was no one to be trifled with. Two words that would perfectly signify her disdain for him.

"You're late."

THE COWBOY'S MAIL ORDER BRIDE

by

Kit Morgan

Libby Blue lived in the shadow of her sister's accomplishments. Bonnie, the oldest, excelled at all things domestic and was the smartest of the three. Gwen, the middle sister, excelled at … well, Gwen was beautiful, so she didn't have to excel at much else to get what she wanted. Libby tried as hard as she could to live up to both, but always seemed to fall short. But when Gwen is caught up in a major scandal, their father decides to marry Libby and her sisters off to the most un-eligible bachelors in Beckham to save the family's reputation. Bonnie quickly devises a plan to escape their father's wrath and sets it in motion. Libby might yet have a chance to prove herself! As a Mail-Order Bride!

Walton Dalton had a dream to build an empire. Or in this case, a ranch where he and his two brothers could work hard and love hard. Determined to see his dream come true, he sends for his brothers and they soon join him in Texas to claim the land and begin building. That took care of the 'work' part. But Walton fails to tell his brothers that he already sent for mail-order brides in order to take care of the 'loving' part. Will Nate Dalton become Libby's road to happiness? Or a slow path to misery because she still can't measure up?

EXCERPT

Nate took care of the horses, fed the chickens, and was heading back to the house when he stopped dead in his tracks. What would happen now? She couldn't cook, was frightened, and, as far as he knew, didn't like this whole arrangement. He stood, fists on hips and stared at the soft lantern light coming from the windows. Maybe she was upset because she was so ill-prepared to be a wife. How would he feel if he was in her shoes? But then, what woman becomes a wife and doesn't learn how to cook? What else would she be inept at? What if she couldn't so much as mend a shirt, or wash it for that matter? He couldn't exactly send her back. But then, what if that's exactly what she wanted him to do?

Nate rubbed his chin with his hand. How to handle her… that was the question. Should he be patient, or tell her to get with it? Maybe a little of both? Yet, what right did he have to be so hard on her their first day as husband and wife? She did just travel over a thousand miles to get there and must be plumb tuckered out. If he was any kind of a gentleman, he'd get a tub ready for her, let her have her privacy, then after she felt better, he could see where she really stood. Yes, that's what he'd do. He wouldn't be surprised if he found her passed out from exhaustion.

Sure enough, when he entered the house, she was curled up at one end of the settee, eyes closed, breathing steady and even. He studied her in the lantern light. How was he going to turn this delicate flower into someone capable of defending herself and their land if need be? This was still rough country, and he and his brothers could be gone long hours during the day. She'd be alone all that time, as would her sisters. They might have to do whatever was necessary to defend themselves. Could she shoot a gun? Could she, would she, shoot a man if she had to? He crossed to the stove and pushed the thought aside. He'd worry about teaching her how to shoot later. Right now he figured he'd help make things more comfortable for her. Tomorrow was going to be a long day.

He got a fire in the cook stove going, fetched the tub he used for bathing and set it up in the bedroom. He then went out to the pump, got a couple buckets of water, and poured them into the tub. He then filled the buckets again, and put them on the stove to heat.

While he waited he sat at the kitchen table and stared at the back of the settee. He tried to imagine the two of them sitting there in the evenings after supper in front of the fire. He'd read a book, she'd knit or something. After awhile, they'd maybe get sleepy, then again, maybe not. Nate swallowed hard and stood. He took a few steps in her direction, and gazed at the back of her head resting on the one pillow he had for the living area. Her dark hair was coming loose from its pins, and a long tendril escaped, spilling over the arm of the settee. He went to her, reached down, and touched the silken lock. His body reacted, and he let go, sucking in a breath as he did. Libby didn't stir, and he sighed in relief.

Once again, he had to concede to her beauty. But how was she going to survive while he was gone all day? He didn't talk much during the ride home, but he listened. Her sister Bonnie asked him if the land around Bart's home would support a vegetable garden come spring. He told her yes, and knew she wanted to have one so there'd be enough food to get them through next winter. She knew how to cook and preserve food, a good thing in these parts. Bart was one lucky son of a …

Libby moaned in her sleep. Nate froze. He sucked in another breath, and slowly backed away. He should wake her now, get her something to eat, then leave her to bathe.

He went back to the kitchen. He had some cold bacon from his breakfast left, and a few biscuits. They would have to do for supper. He cut a biscuit in half, slapped a couple pieces of bacon on it, then went to wake his sleeping wife.

He gave her shoulder a shake, and almost jumped when she popped up with a yelp. "Whoa, there," he said in a soft voice. "I didn't mean to scare ya."

She stared at him, her mouth half-open. "Wha… what?" She glanced around the cabin. "What happened?"

"You dozed off. Here, I rustled us up

something to eat," he said and handed her the biscuit. She looked at it, then at him. "What is it?"

"Just eat, you'll need something in your belly or you'll be worthless in the morning."

"Worthless?" she whispered. "I see." She took the biscuit from him, studied it, and took a small bite.

"I done fixed you a bath. You can get cleaned up before you turn in. I don't imagine you'd want to sleep in a clean bed unless you're the same."

She raised her eyes to his. "Understood," she said through gritted teeth.

Good grief! What was ailing her now? "I'll be out in the barn." He went to the stove, checked the water, then using a couple of dishrags, plucked the buckets off and added them to the tub in the bedroom. Maybe after she got cleaned up she wouldn't be so... well, whatever it was she was being! All he knew was he didn't care for it. If she was going to be the kind of woman that was hard to please, then this arrangement wasn't going to be to his liking. At least not until she learned what was what.

"I'm going to the barn. I'll be back in an hour." He didn't mean to slam the door on his way out, but he did. Some wedding night this was turning out to be.

Made in the USA
Columbia, SC
24 August 2022